Below the Falls

Stories

Ross McMeekin

thirtywestph.com

This is a work of fiction. Names, characters, businesses, places,
events, locales, and incidents are either the products of the
author's imagination or used in a fictitious manner. Any
resemblance to actual persons, living or dead, or actual
events is purely coincidental.

ISBN-13: 979-8-9895422-1-5
Cover design by Josh Dale
Edited by Chanel Martins
Author Photo by Ross McMeekin
Printed in the U.S.A.

For more titles and inquiries, please visit:
www.thirtywestph.com

For Naomi and Gus

Table of Contents

Below the Falls

Below the Falls

Through his good eye, the boy could just make out the passing trees, boulders, and bushes in the faint light of the moon, which was veiled by a river of mist coasting a dozen yards overhead. A gust of morning wind through the river valley grazed the bare skin of the boy's hands. He pulled them into the sleeves of his parka and crouched low against the bow of the drift boat. His father sat above in the crossbar seat, crowned by a headlamp, correcting their drift with his large wooden oars.

His father's headlamp shot a spotlight here and there along the river and the bank and occasionally on the boy. His father liked that the air smelled of damp earth and vegetation. He also liked to hear the uninterrupted sounds of the wind, waking birds, weed stalks rubbing together in the shallows, and the occasional gurgles and slurps of slow-moving water. These smells and sounds reminded him that he existed. Sometimes during his long days working the assembly line, as he rehashed the same blunt action over and over, it felt as if he did not.

The boy lived with his mother in an apartment in the city. His mother worked at a shipping warehouse most days and as a waitress at a chain diner two nights a week. The boy took the metro bus to parochial school and back during the school year. He was responsible for the preparation of dinner and of the washing of dishes and clothes during the evenings his mother worked.

The boy spent one weekend each month with his

father, who lived two hours north. His mother occasionally told the boy that, despite her wishes, he had to visit his father. They had no choice. It was the law. Every month, upon his return, she urged the boy to tell her everything that had happened, even if there didn't seem to be anything worth telling.

The boy was very small for his age, and the way he crouched deep into the bow of the boat diminished his stature even more.

His father tried his best not to blame the boy and his mother for his size, but it was difficult because he believed that, had he been allowed to stick around, the boy would have turned out more substantial.

The boat shifted and rocked as the boy and his father switched places.

The boy felt the warmth left by his father on the seat. He palmed the oars and felt the warmth there, too.

Whenever the boy thought of his father, the first image that came into his mind was the domed curvature of his eyes and the hawkish way they protruded from their sockets. Even in pictures, his look could startle.

There on the river, the boy couldn't see his father's eyes, only the cool glow the headlamp lent his father's breath, which twisted and spun in front of his lips before dissolving. But those eyes never left the boy's imagination; the figments remained fixed, even in the dark.

His father pulled a leather case from beneath a storage shelf below the gunwale on the port side of the drift boat. He unzipped the case and slid out a rifle. The beam of the headlamp searched up and down the length of it, illuminating its structure with light.

Though the boy had never before seen a rifle in person—and he suspected his mother would not approve—the rifle itself was not the object that most captured his attention; it was the brass shells. In the light of his father's headlamp, they shined like so many pieces of gold. Such beauty encased what rifles hurled through the air. Glossy gems held the stuff that plugged holes into skin and hide.

The boy's father had many memories of his own deceased father, but the beatings stood out. His own father, when drunk, struck him and his sisters with his hands and his knees and his cane and his belt and his shoes and, once, with a ceramic lamp.

The time with the lamp had left a crescent-shaped scar on the back of his head around which hair still refused to grow. The scar was on the back of his head because, at the time of the blow, he was crouched over his younger sister to protect her.

He tried hard to make sense of the old man, but couldn't, even when he ended up working in the same factory, drinking the same beer, and sipping the same bourbon from the same flask at his lunch break. Understanding remained out of reach, even when, like his own father, he married a woman who wanted to save him from himself and had children he hoped would change him in the ways he felt he should change.

Decades before, one fine morning of a September in his childhood, the boy's father and his own father went out fishing before dawn. There, the boy's father learned how best to catch salmon. If one were to come upon them unawares in the dark, using the headlamp as a guide, they would fire a shot just above the fish's snout. The rifle shot would serve as a concussive blast, and the salmon would float to the surface, stunned.

That it was illegal to do this, that they agreed no one else should know, that they made up a plausible story should they be questioned about poaching—all this only made the time between the two more special.

The jet stream of mist above the river had now sunk to eye level, and the boy, through his good eye, watched its small shimmering beads glisten in the light of his father's headlamp. He felt the moisture dampen his lips but not his cheeks, which were chilled numb.

His father's outline stood in the haze and lumen of the headlamp, butt of the rifle against one shoulder, fingers floating over the trigger, other hand outstretched, palm up, steadying the barrel.

The spotlight of his father's lamp followed slow, searching arcs across the surface of the river. Where it landed, the water turned shallow green, like that of half-brewed tea.

His father fired.

The salmon floated toward the boat, white belly breaching the surface just as the rifle report ceased echoing along the canyon. The boy's father reached out, sunk the net into the water, and then hoisted it up, pausing for a moment before setting it down in the hull so that the boy could see the shuddering arc of the salmon bulge in the bottom of the fluorescent green netting.

Chinook, said the boy's father. See the mouth? That's how you tell it's a hen.

This was verbatim what his own father had said to him years earlier.

The boy nodded.

In the light of the headlamp, the boy's father noticed the opaque film covering the boy's fake eye. The boy had lost the eye years before when his father had struck him with the palm of his hand because the boy had been using some of his prized baseball cards for spoke flaps on his bicycle.

Since the event, the boy's father often reminded himself that it was an accident and that it had occurred while delivering a punishment that was justified—a punishment meant to teach the boy a lesson every child needed to learn.

The boy's father reminded himself of this often, because the image of the boy's real eye, loose against his cheek, appeared often in his mind, and the shortness of breath accompanying the image wouldn't go away without a struggle.

The chrome, green, and blue salmon dazzled in the light of the headlamp but gave off a faint, harsh smell somewhere between asparagus and gasoline. The boy reached out and touched its silvery skin near the tail. It felt smooth, a little slimy. Little lumps lined the white scaling near the posterior fin, resembling little pearls.

His father coughed into his fist a few times, then caught his breath. Finally, he said: Sea lice. This hen's fresh from the salt. Maybe even came up yesterday. He then wiped the bugs from the salmon with his finger and flicked them into the water.

When a moth became trapped inside their apartment in the city, the boy's mother would capture it between her palms and release it out the window.

His father pulled a sheath from the front pocket of his jeans and slid out a bone-handled knife. With the blade, he pierced the fish's skull.

The boy felt there was something brutal about the sound. It wasn't a sound he had heard before, and now the boy wished he never had. He felt certain he would hear it in his dreams.

The boy watched the fish in its death throes. Gills bleeding, the salmon opened its mouth and wiggled. Its pupils widened beneath the glow of the headlamp, and its body curved as if stretching.

The officer wore large aviator glasses that reflected the pullout adjacent to the river in a distorted way. Wedged beneath his armpit was a notepad. He spun a pencil in his fingers. He strolled around the boat, peering inside. He set his notebook on the ground and leaned deep for a closer look. His feet nearly left the ground.

The officer exhaled audibly and returned to his feet. He picked up his notebook and flipped a few pages. He took off his glasses and slid them between two buttons of his tan, collared shirt.

Let's start with your licenses, he said.

The boy had been taught by his mother not to lie. The boy had been taught by his father not to lie. The boy had heen taught in parochial school not to lie. This left the boy unprepared to lie. He was willing, but without practice.

A gust of canyon wind rattled the papers in the father's hand. He stretched the papers flat against his knees and finished reading. When finished, he folded them up and slid them into his breast pocket where they stuck up nearly to his collar.

The tires of the officer's tan pickup truck spun gravel as he left the parking lot.

The father and the boy sat next to each other in the cab of the truck as they drove along the empty highway, towing the drift boat behind. Neither of them said a word. The boy felt as though his lungs didn't work—that they wouldn't fill up. He tried his best not to reveal this.

His father's chapped lips wrapped snug around a cigarette while his teeth worked out something behind it. In rhythm with his grinding, a vein popped up and disappeared on the side of his forehead. His pronounced eyes strained from their sockets.

He settled his foot onto the breaks, palmed the gearshift down a few notches, and slowed onto the shoulder of the highway until they were stopped.

The boy picked up his fake eye from the footwell of the truck, licked his fingers, and began to rub the eyeball clean in his palm. It felt warm to the touch.

His father said, I'm sorry. I didn't mean—

The boy interrupted him and said, It's okay.

The boy said this because it did feel okay, now that the

ridge along his eyebrow throbbed, now that the inside of his empty eye socket was itchy, now that the side of his face felt hot and feverish. The world felt somehow righted. He didn't understand why, but there was now more room in his lungs to fill with breath.

The father reached over and hugged the boy.

The boy leaned in.

The salmon lay still in the back.

Breakup Sketch

Attorney Meredith Browning's husband of five years, Drew Baxter, an emerging star in stand-up and sketch comedy, now on the second season of the eponymous sitcom based on his life—both their lives—walked naked into the kitchen. He sat down adjacent to her at the square island in their Greenwich Village apartment and stared.

"Morning," she said, reading the *New York Times* on her laptop and chewing a spoonful of yogurt mixed with sliced strawberries and slivered almonds. She glanced up. "What the fuck?"

With a thick green marker, he'd drawn branches stemming wide from the dark red scar down the center of his chest, left from emergency open heart surgery six months earlier. He'd sketched a tree. "I've made a nicer home for my heart."

He was always so droll—she usually found that attractive—but it was difficult to laugh. The sight of the scar still conjured flashes of memory from when she'd almost lost him and the time she'd taken off from work to nurse him back to health.

"Get it?" he asked.

"Are you high?" On mornings he had no responsibilities, he liked to wake-and-bake. The previous night, he'd been snoring, so he'd slept in the spare room they planned to someday become a nursery. They'd already discussed what color to paint an accent wall when they were ready—which meant when *he* was ready, because she'd been ready for two years. A week ago, at the Cellar, he'd tried out a bit about the accent wall and his parental indecision. He refused to talk about his act before performances, so she never had a say in what he wrote. Their life was on display, an unauthorized biography written by him, alone.

"Merry Christmas, Meredith," he said, holding out a yellow marker. "I'll let you put up the star."

"It's March."

He coughed for a moment, and she flinched, worried the cough might become something more. Since the surgery, sometimes when he coughed, it hurt, and he would wheeze and curl up around his chest like a pill bug. While vacationing upstate, he'd once picked a pill bug from beneath a rock, wiped it off, and ate it, just to provoke her. He smiled as he did it, as if he was fulfilling a dare at the expense of something helpless.

He recovered from the coughing. "Your loss, Rebel Wilson. You know she studied to be a lawyer? Had a bit about it. You could open a practice with her." He slid the cap from the yellow marker, drew a ragged star above the tree on his chest, then hurried to their bedroom, presumably to look in the mirror. "It's a mess," he said from bedroom. "Like me." He walked back into the kitchen. "Messy star. You could say it's a self-portrait."

"It's flattering."

"Now rise, counsel. And pull up your shirt."

"I'm not in the mood."

"I don't want to have sex. I want to draw on you."

She turned back to the laptop. "You're high."

"Okay, I'll be serious. Meredith, this is serious. Trust me."

He looked sincere. He only got this way occasionally, and it was always for something important. Usually he'd just play sincere, to goad her into becoming the role in one of his jokes. She was one of his characters—the snide, killjoy wife. Since he'd become famous, sometimes she worried she was becoming more and more like her role in his act, if only because that's what people assumed of her. When someone relates to you as if you're acerbic and uptight, you either have to go along with it or make the effort to prove their assumptions wrong. Tiring.

"It's not a joke," he said. "Trust me. You'll like it."

"You have to promise me. I'm not playful right now. Like, not at all. This meeting at ten for the civil case isn't casual."

"Trust me. You can trust me."

"Fine." She stood and lifted her shirt.

"Hold still." He leaned over and began drawing a large square around her belly button in purple. The pen felt cool on her skin, and she shivered. The sound the pen made was humiliating. It was like he was writing a joke. She imagined her belly swelling from pregnancy and the ink soaking through her skin to what curled inside her womb. It struck her that, though she loved this broken man, she no longer wanted to have his baby. She could handle being a source of material for him, a recurring bit in his act, but she couldn't allow her child to grow up as one. This very moment might end up on Netflix.

Before he could finish his sketch, she pulled down her shirt.

"Wait! I need to add the bow. Trust me, you'll love it."

"Is that marker permanent?"

He glanced down at it. "I hope so."

"Fuck, Drew."

He stepped back and set the marker on a stack of

magazines. "No, no, I get it. That was too much. I should explain myself."

"It doesn't matter. I have to get ready for this meeting. But we need to talk. Tonight."

"Trust me. I'll be quick. So I was drawing a present on your belly. A gift. And it's March, like you said. And nine months from now it will be December. Christmas is in December. So if you get pregnant in March, we'll have a baby in December. So I'm the tree, and you hold the present."

She sat back down.

"This heart thing changed me, Meredith. I'm asking you to make a baby with me."

Permanent markers eventually wore off. "I know."

Tonight We Are Kings

"Peanuts," I say. "That's all I want you to think about." My new friend keeps trying to talk about serious things, like science, like how the number of genes that can shape a person's face are limited enough statistically that we all have multiple twins on Earth. I just hope to once again feel what it's like to really want something. I grab the plastic bottle from him and swallow a finger or two of vodka.

"Peanuts, like the comic and the Christmas special?" he says, popping a nut into his mouth, shell and all. He chews it and spits out some gristle, but a little works its way onto his lower lip and stays there. "With the trumpets?"

He means Charlie Brown. "No. And it was a flugelhorn, not a trumpet."

"A flugelhorn is a trumpet."

"And salt is pepper," I say.

"You need to meet Pepper." He holds out both fists and makes a humping motion.

"You need to think about peanuts," I say again.

"I've already thought about them."

"So?"

"They give me heartburn." He pops another into his mouth, chews, spits, and takes a long drink of vodka. Once he's done, the bit of shell on his lower lip is gone.

"Pepper gives me heartburn," I say.

"She gives me heartburn, too." He laughs and does the phantom hump again.

I can't see Staples Center yet, but I can see its glow. People are starting to file toward the hockey game. Cars slouch by. I wish I had tickets. I want to see an Anže Kopitar slapshot.

"I'm going to ask him," says my new friend, pointing to a guy in a vintage Oilers jersey jogging alone across the street. He's really tall, and I recognize his face. Is he famous? He's something. I can't place him. "Hey, mister."

The tall man nods and slows down. He's not famous; he's familiar. I wonder if we went to high school together. Maybe he was an officer. I picture him in uniform, but nothing's certain.

"Question for you," my new friend says to the man.

He waves him off. "I don't have any change."

"No, no, no," my new friend says. "We need to know a question—we need to ask you a question."

The guy checks his watch and says, "Okay, shoot." His nose has a notch in the middle. Maybe that's why he's familiar.

"Is a flugelhorn a trumpet or something else?" my new friend asks.

"I'd guess it's a trumpet."

Before we can respond, he jogs off toward the arena.

My new friend grins. "See? One in the same. One in the same!" He grabs the bottle back and takes a swig.

"He said he only guessed."

"But look at him. He would be a guy who knows. Did you see his hair? That's hair that's been to the symphony."

"He said he guessed," I say, "but whatever." I grab the bottle back. The vodka doesn't tickle my throat this time.

"He was an okay dude. He was okay."

I realize we've stopped walking when a family with a mother and daughter holding hands walks past us, using the edge of the sidewalk and a bit of the street to give us a wide berth. I deserve the space, more than they know, more than my new friend knows. "Let's keep moving."

"How long have I known you, Dennis?" he asks as we walk.

I still can't remember his name. I look down at my watch. I don't have a watch. "I don't know, forty-five minutes?"

"It feels like forty-six."

"What's that supposed to mean?"

"We're like old pals," he says. "Sheesh. It's a compliment."

"I thought you were saying you were tired of me," I say, which feels truer than anything I've said in a long time.

My new friend stops and puts his hand on my shoulder, gets his face right up into mine. He breathes through his nose. I can smell peanuts and rot. "People who get tired of people are just tired, man. Not tired of you. Just tired."

I nod and back away. I don't think he's right, but I'd rather pretend so he'll give me some space. The sadness feels sweet. I take another swig of vodka and close my eyes so I can concentrate.

~

The arena is just up the street on the left. I can see the glitter, the flash. They even have one of those big, rotating searchlights like the ones we had on base. "Let's hang out for a bit," I say. It will be nice to be in a crowd. We can watch everyone and have something to talk about.

"I have a philosophical question for you," says my new

friend. He begins snapping his fingers along to some beat in his head. "Why aren't we in the National Hockey League?"

A dozen people surge past us on their way to the game. We're now just outside, on the veranda, or the patio. Whatever; it's nice. I see an Arizona Coyotes uniform, then another. I'd forgotten they had a team. I didn't think Arizona had any water, much less ice.

"There are a thousand reasons," I say.

"There's only one," he says.

"We suck at skating," I say.

"What does that have to do with it? Goalies don't have to skate."

This isn't true, but I want to be done. "Just tell me."

"We'll get there," he says.

"I don't want to guess," I say. This isn't philosophy. I'd rather just watch people than be led down some line of questions that ends with a trick. "I'm too tired."

"It's not skating," he says and rubs his chin, watching the searchlight wander.

"Fine. The reason we're not in the NHL isn't skating," I say. I don't mention that, in my childhood in Minnesota, I was a fine skater. In fact, I was a junior prospect at left wing in high school. Scouts showed up to games, but I wasn't good enough. It wasn't for lack of hard work; I always knew I had to make the most of what talent I had. It just wasn't in the cards, but I still wanted to be something—something more than what my shitty grades and small-time connections would make me—so I chased it and enlisted.

"Okay. Time's up," says my friend. "Do you want to know why?"

I wait.

"We're not Canadian. To be in the NHL, you must be Canadian. That's the ticket. You can do and be everything else, but you must have Mountie blood."

This is tiring. I no longer feel close to my new friend. I can't tell how old he is. He might be sixty, but he might be forty. "What's your point?"

"We're American. That's why we could never be in the NHL."

"That's the stupidest thing I've ever heard."

"You must have been around some geniuses." He takes a drink from the bottle. I can tell I've hurt his feelings. That's another thing that always happens. "How long have I known you now, Dennis?" he asks me.

I peel up my sleeve and show him my empty wrist. "I don't know. An hour."

My new friend removes his cap and sets it on the ground in front of him, open for business. "It still feels like forty-six minutes." He toasts me with the vodka and takes a swig.

I'm about to apologize when he interrupts me.

"Relax man," he says. "Have a peanut."

I don't respond because a face distracts me. Another face I recognize, another I can't place. This time, it's a guy who's with a woman. They are taking pictures of each other with the arena in the background. He turns this way and that, and I still know his face.

"It's better to be American in some ways," my new friend says. He's been talking this entire time, but I haven't been listening. The couple has already taken pictures with the statues of Oscar de la Hoya and Wayne Gretzky. "Just in case anyone tries to invade, you know?"

Now the couple is walking toward us. They stop at the statue of Magic Johnson.

"Trust me," my new friend says. "What are you, anyway?"

"What do you mean?" I say, still looking at the couple.

"What nationality?"

"I'm Irish."

"No, you're not. You're American. You were born here, right? And anyways, if you're white, people assume you're American, but if you're Korean, even if you're born here, you're still Korean. Even if you served. Trust me."

"I thought you were Chinese," I say.

"Exactly. Tarzana, born and raised, but somehow not American. Still, I'd rather be Canadian than..."

I stop listening because the guy I can't place has finished posing for his picture with Magic, and now he's looking at me again. We make eye contact. It's unsettling. He nudges his girlfriend. Now she's looking at me, too.

"I know this guy," I say.

My new friend turns around and sees the couple near the Magic Johnson bronze, looking at me.

"Those two?" he says. "See, he's American. Not Icelandic or whatever."

"I know him," I say, but from where, I can't for the life of me remember. I take a drink of vodka and blink to bring his face in and out of focus. It's no use.

People around us are talking. It has become crowded. Fans hurry by. The game must be starting soon.

"Hey!" says my new friend, waving to the blondes. "My friend says he knows you. My friend Dennis says." He turns and points to me.

"I wondered if that was you," says the guy. He comes

closer, and I recognize him. I also recognize his voice, but it's still unclear from where.

"Me too," I say.

He looks at the bottle of vodka in my hand. He looks at it for longer than just a glance, so I hold it up to him. "Want some?"

He shakes his head in disgust. "Don't do that, Dennis. This isn't you."

I have heard him say something like this before, and then I realize that this man was my sponsor when I tried to get sober awhile back. I stopped returning his calls once I decided I wasn't going to return his calls. I wanted to quit, but there are things you want to do, and then there are things you're going to do. My tongue feels big. "I'm sorry. I didn't recognize you until now."

"Come back to the meetings," he says. "This isn't a coincidence. Tomorrow at six, we'll be at the Y."

His girlfriend looks bewildered.

"Holy shit!" says my new friend. "Is this guy your sponsor or something?" Then my new friend is cracking up. People make room around us. I feel out of breath.

"You're welcome to come, too," says my old sponsor to my new friend.

I wish my old sponsor would leave. I can tell his girlfriend wishes the same.

"Nah," says my new friend. "I've already been through all the steps." He grabs the vodka bottle from me. "This step is called love."

~

We're down the street from Staples Center, panhandling next to a strip club lit by a neon silhouette of a woman with cats twining around her high heels. Clubs are some of the best places to fundraise; a lot of the people leaving are looking for a way to feel better about themselves.

"That guy thought he knew you," says my new friend, still fired up about my old sponsor. "I hate it when people think they know you."

"He didn't know me," I say, thinking, *neither do you.*

"I didn't think so," says my new friend. He pulls up the arm of his t-shirt and shows me a tattoo of the war eagle. "Do you see this?"

"Yeah, I see it."

"People shouldn't talk like they know," he says.

That tat doesn't mean you know me, either, I think. A group of men in suits walks out of the club, laughing. I don't recognize them, but the whole deal with the sponsor has made me a little shy, so I pull down my stocking cap and hold out a keg cup.

"We are two vets full of love and in desperate need of affection," says my friend. His name has now emerged from the mess in my head. It's Jack. Of course, it's Jack.

"Sponsor us toward a lap dance."

The men pretend we aren't there. I drink a finger while Jack continues to shit on my old sponsor, who was really an okay guy just doing what he thought was right, like most of the rest of us. But the thing about this world? It seems like the more certain you are that you're right, the more damage you're likely to do.

There are a few Kings fans scurrying past us, late to the game, dressed in black and silver. They are fuzzy around the edges and remind me of winter in Minnesota. I couldn't live in Minnesota anymore. It's not where I belong. There aren't enough distractions, and it's too cold. When I was a kid, I would ride my bike around with the windchill at forty-five below. I'd get so cold I couldn't feel my lips or cheeks. I remember once my bike got a flat, and I had to walk home from hockey. All the sweat on my feet froze. When I got home, it was all right, but the next day, my toes puffed up with blisters that looked like deer droppings. After that, I had trouble feeling the cold. The itchiness and pain were no longer there to warn me, so when I was overseas, I'd sometimes take off my boots and find a bloody mess.

I realize this is important—deep—and I'm about to tell Jack when I realize he's close to me again, hands on my shoulders, breath swampy. I can see the individual wisps of hair that together make his mustache and goatee. He snorts like a bull. He's angry and serious. Some people get this way when they're drunk: they thrust all the sympathy they wish they had for themselves onto you.

"Don't listen to people like that," he says. "People like that don't understand why they aren't in the NHL."

I laugh hard enough that I have to sit down right there on the sidewalk outside the club, with the lights and people whirring all around me. It takes some time to calm down and catch my breath.

Jack grabs me by my wrist and pulls me to my feet. I feel closer to him now than I've felt to anyone in a long time.

"I love Wayne Gretzky," I say to him, and I fucking mean it just like I fucking meant to quit drinking. I'm glad I'm someplace crowded, someplace where people are having fun, where people are on their way to cheer for something as meaningless as hockey. It makes me happy to know that men will make millions skating around on an ice rink inside Staples Center, trying to sling a puck into a net, huge crowds cheering them on. There's no guilt in what they do. No questions. Their heroism is so simple.

"Gretzky!" Jack yells, spinning around, looking for him. He pulls a few bucks from his cup and nods back toward Staples. "Let's go back and see how the Great One is doing."

I look up. It feels like the sexy neon sign is buzzing just for me. "No. He's busy. Let's go inside and see how long it takes them to realize we're broke."

"Stash it," he says, and I wrap the brown paper bag around the bottle and tuck it into the garbage can outside so we can pick it up later.

"Tonight we are kings," Jack says.

~

I wake up, and we're under the Santa Monica Pier. It feels like we're in some Gothic church from a world I've only seen in pictures, but the pillars are bare wood and smell of salt and tar. I close my eyes and can hear the waves crashing. By counting the period of time between each of their roars, I can tell they're from thousands of miles away, probably what's left of a huge storm way out in the North Pacific.

Jack is next to me, also lying on the sand. "What time is it?" I ask.

"We have too many memorials of the dead," he says.

I open my eyes again and look around. It's night. I can

see the moon but no stars. Lights from the pier and the city erased them. A few folks are still sitting on towels on the beach. Others are walking along the boardwalk. It must still be early.

"Gretzky is alive," says Jack. "He's probably back in Staples Center as we speak. We celebrate him while his blood is still warm."

"I want to see the stars," I tell him. Above us are dead trees. It occurs to me how lucky we are to even have trees left to kill, but I stop myself, because that's philosophy, and no philosophy ever made anyone smile. "Five bucks says I know more constellations."

"You don't have five bucks," says Jack. He's still lying in the sand, and he's right, but I do know my constellations: Orion, the hunter; Cassiopeia, the queen; Perseus, the hero. I learned them all overseas, watched them burn at night. They made me feel small. A lot of people stateside talk fondly of humbling experiences, which tells me they've never truly been humbled.

"Sex begins with the continents," says Jack.

I realize that Jack's probably been following me because I don't say much and, in that way, resemble an audience. But now I'm more than willing to give him what he wants. "Explain."

"Think about South America and Africa. They fit like a lock and key." He puts his arm around my shoulder. He smells terrible, but so do I.

"But then they broke apart," I say.

Jack points up at an airplane banking around the bay, en route to LAX. "And now we have airplanes."

~

The bus takes us back to Staples Center. The game is over, and all the fans are walking from the arena. Relief is in the air now instead of the pregame tension. It's Friday night, and the Kings have won. Meanwhile, we've cruised the city and killed a bottle. I feel good, but my lips are dry, so we're back to fundraising on the patio.

"We are the champions, my friends," Jack hollers, holding out his Dodgers hat.

The lights around us sway. A mother and small boy walk by. The little boy has his t-shirt tucked into his jeans and his hands tucked into his pockets. He stares at me in that way children do before they understand it's impolite. I remember a time when I was a kid, riding the escalator up to the second floor of a shopping center near downtown Minneapolis with my father. At the top of the escalator stood a homeless guy with layers of clothing and piles of hair, looking disoriented and grim. My father muttered down to me not to look at him. I obeyed, and we walked past, and nothing happened. Later I asked him why he said not to look at the man. My father replied that if you lock eyes with a guy like him, he'll follow you. Or chase you.

"You look tired," says Jack's voice. "No one is tired of you. I told you that."

I push him and he stumbles. He keeps making us go backward in time. I point at his face. "Why do you have to do that?"

"Relax, man. I'm just saying."

"Leave me alone."

There are heads swerving around, in and out of focus. I stumble over and sit down beneath the statue of Wayne Gretzky. My sponsor is probably out there in the crowd, watching, knowing. He's the type of guy who looks in the mirror and knows exactly what to make of what he sees.

I lie back on the patio, rest my heels up against the base of the statue and look. I know that above us burn the stars, but they've been washed out by the arena lights. If I could sit down with Wayne, I'd ask him what it's like being a hero with medals, statues, and photographs. I'd ask him what getting everything he'd ever wanted cost him.

Jack starts tying my shoe as it rests up against the statue. "I know this place down by the airport. There's a guy who's usually there." He pulls tight the final loop. "You remind me of him. I mean, he reminds me of you."

"What's his name?"

"We're old pals." He pats me on the shoe and nods that we should go.

I take a deep breath and one last look. The statue of the Great One presides over us, like the king he is. I wonder how he's doing, whether he's still got anything hot and burning in his gut. Here, he looks calm and content, arm raised, saluting the crowd, but anyone can do that convincingly if they really need to. It's kind of crazy that another five guys who look just like him are walking the Earth this very moment. Maybe some of them are heroes, too.

Small Fiery Bloom

One morning, in the last winter of her long life, a widow sat by a window overlooking acres of fallow farmland cloaked in deep snow. A fire grumbled and hissed in the wood stove behind her, a cup of coffee cooled on the armrest, and in her lap sat a plate of peppered eggs.

She took a bite and glanced up. On the deck outside stood a bird she'd never laid eyes on before. Its plumage was raven-black and its size that of a starling, though it was clearly neither species: on its chest, in the place below its neck where one might hang a medallion, gleamed a feathered patch of turquoise.

As if perceiving an audience, the bird puffed its wings into a black oval disc and agitated its feathers so that the color pattern resembled two turquoise eyes and a morose, turquoise mouth. The bird proceeded to bob and jerk on its needle legs, which appeared even more diminutive amidst the broad display. While dancing, it erupted in a series of sharp, timed clicks clearly audible through the windowpane.

The bird continued to dance in fits and starts. The widow watched in astonishment. Meanwhile, an unseasonable warmth blossomed inside of her. She absently touched the tips of her fingers to her lips, then moved them to her cheeks, which flushed at her own touch.

Soon, the dance came to an end, and the bird re-assumed its common shape. Briefly, it stood erect, eyeing the widow, before hopping a few times to the edge of the deck and taking flight, a quick black puff flitting low across the snowy plain.

The widow stayed seated for some time, hoping the bird would return. Once her coffee got cold, she left the window, creaked up the stairs, and opened the door to her deceased husband's office. Inside were stacks of yellowed paper and dozens of antiquated textbooks—a mess she hadn't touched in the decade since his passing. It took until early afternoon, but finally, her excavation yielded a glossy, hardbound avian desk reference with an illustration of her visitor: the male Lophorina superba, a Bird of Paradise native to the South Pacific.

Its performance was a mating display.

~

The visitor returned the next day and the next. It arrived each morning for three weeks and danced while the widow sipped her coffee, ate her peppered eggs, and quietly swooned from behind the pane. A new vigor, absent for decades, permeated every aspect of her life. She organized her husband's neglected belongings—moth-eaten clothes, brittle papers and books—filling the attic with objects that held value and triggered memories. The rest she consumed in a massive, two-day blaze set just out of reach of the barn. She administered a thorough abstersion of the house with lemon juice. She sanded and stained the faded wood floors, slats, beams, and pillars of the house's interior, unmasking the deep reds of its cedar bones. Callouses formed over the widow's hands, and with them returned the former mettle of her posture, as well as the fortitude of the home she'd helped build nearly half a century before.

While righting the harvest of those bleak years, she spotted her old easel which was packed tightly in the back of a storage shed attached to the outside of the barn. She scattered the mice and swept through spider webs before wrestling it out from behind decaying tarps and half-used cans of paint and varnish. She spit into her palm and wiped away the dust from one of the easel's legs, revealing the fine grains of its wood—her husband had refashioned it from a cracked bed frame he'd found abandoned by the side of the road.

There, in the field outside the barn, she scrubbed the easel down with snow, then took it inside and applied graphite to its joints. She spread it out in front of a large, multi-sectioned window in what had been her husband's office. She drove six hours into the city to purchase a few canvases, brushes, and tubes of oil paint. She'd majored in art at the small women's college she'd attended in the fifties, but she'd let her talent atrophy with the kids and then become buried during her husband's long decline and passing.

After her full days of labor, the widow painted long into the winter nights, taking sips of cognac between brush strokes, listening to the warm fuzz and crackle of the old needle on her record player as it skimmed across the vinyl of her youth.

~

One morning, she walked to the window with her peppered eggs and coffee in hand to find the bird already outside. It wasn't dancing on the deck, but struggling on its side, as if in the throes of a bad dream. She dropped her wares and rushed out the door. Cold wet crept through her skirt as she knelt and cupped her palms beneath the visitor. She pressed her thumbs into its breast and could feel its heart pattering in panic. The bird blinked its eyes and wiped them with the edges of its wings.

The widow ran the bird inside and up the stairs to her office. Out of breath, she held the bird upright so that it might see itself in the dozen paintings spread across the wall, each of them capturing a moment of the strange, elegant dance it performed every morning. She moved the bird closer, then further away, from side to side, so that it might see itself as she saw it, from every remarkable angle, in every beautiful pose. Through her fingers, the widow felt the bird's heart begin to slow, until finally its talons flexed, relaxed, and stopped moving altogether. She gazed into what had been its full black eyes, now emptied.

Carrying the corpse, the widow moved slowly downstairs, nursing a dull pain blooming in her hip born from her urgent flight up the staircase. She limped into the sitting room and set the body next to the fireplace on a stack of newspapers. She sat for a time and studied it. Then she got up and stabbed the charred wood in the fireplace with the poker until a small flame peeked out from beneath. She stacked four large cedar halves on top of the iron crosshairs. The flames began to crackle and creep up through the dry wood.

The widow winced as she retrieved a heavy, wrought iron skillet from the kitchen, one used for pies and casseroles and cobblers. She caught her breath as she knelt down and placed the bird in the center of the skillet. She paused for one last look at the bird before setting the heavy lid over it with a clang. With both hands on the long handle, she placed the skillet on top of the blazing cedar halves.

After a few deep breaths, she sat down in her chair and waited, the knees of her skirt still wet from snow, her peppered eggs uneaten, coffee lukewarm.

~

For eight hours she tended the fire. Then the widow layered her hands with towels, removed the skillet from the flames, then took the lid from off the top. Inside lay a small gathering of ash where the bird had been, only a few thimbles' worth in all. The mound was so small and plain. *All flickering*, she thought, *eventually gives way to smoke.*

With a small basting brush, she coaxed the ash onto a plate. Then she spun open the top of the bottle of pepper she used each morning for her eggs and gently swept the ash inside where it formed a light layer on top of the darker-hued pepper.

The widow twisted shut the tin top of the pepper bottle and shook it and shook it, until finally she could no longer recognize the difference.

First Rain

When no rain had fallen for sixty days and all the fine bits of rubber and oil and dirt and ash and exhaust had mashed together beneath three months of hurtling sedans and semis; when said dregs had caulked every cranny and fracture of the highway asphalt, and the composite mat had grown so slow and complete it was invisible on the road like how cigarette smoke colors white walls and no one notices until a fresh paint stroke makes stripes; that's when we decided to leave the restaurant for home.

Then it rained. Showers fell on the highway and rain pecked at the grit. Beneath our tires, the wet seeped in and expanded that stale cracker, melting it back to batter. That's when I clicked on the windshield wipers and rested the palm of my hand on your thigh.

You burrowed into my shoulder as if you hadn't said earlier that it was finished between us, again. You closed your eyes. It was late and you were drunk. You smacked your lips, and I thought of how tomorrow the surfers would sit on the roofs of their vans and in the flatbeds of their trucks and curse the rain because of all the mess it carried into the ocean. How they'd drink and hypothesize how many days it would take for the risk of infection to sink low enough to justify a session. Then, after enough unclaimed sets, they'd paddle out anyway.

Then I thought of that overlook where you could sometimes see whales, the one with canyons to spare, covered in wildflowers, thirsty for rain. I was stupid and sentimental. I thought that maybe what we needed was a good storm, even though it might be terrible in the moment. I almost woke you to tell you to smell how sharp the air was, how it could cut like paper.

I looked back at the road and saw that our car was about to hit a deer. I braked and our tires spun free over that paper-deep mash. No purchase. You sucked in a breath and spread your hands wide against the dash while I gripped the steering wheel, and we spun. I couldn't stop us.

There was no accident, no wreck, nothing. Just a brief, more exciting way to spend the time, with rain as the only witness, gossiping on the roof. I apologized and took you home.

The Island

Owen watched Aubrey press her palm into a thick patch of speckled moss girdling the trunk of an old Douglas fir. The move was gentle and precise, how a mime might seek an invisible wall, and he couldn't help but imagine her locked up in some dark basement, kidnapped, as he suspected she'd been as a child.

"Feel," she said of the moss. "It's so soft you could sleep on it." She flinched and looked up. "Rain."

The canopy was thick with greens and browns and had been dripping since they reached the small, uninhabited island that morning. They'd set off from Friday Harbor a few days before to tour the San Juan Islands by kayak. The trip was her idea. When crossing deep channels, he found himself fearing broad-chested sea lions with swells of blubber on their necks. Then muscular pods of orcas. Rogue waves. Freak storms. Mindless currents. Water so cold that hypothermia took only minutes to set in. Somehow, she found this sort of thing relaxing. Loved it. And he loved her.

They'd left their kayaks on the edge of the forest, bike-locked to a sapling. She'd called the lock absurd, but he could tell that she also found it endearing, as she did most of his other little obsessions. In that way, at least, love made sense: what failed lovers found annoying, true lovers found comic.

"Maybe," he said about the potential rain. "It's tough to tell here in the woods."

Aubrey looked around. Despite the summer warmth, she hugged herself. "It does feel like we're inside."

~

The morning after they'd first slept together, he'd awakened in his downtown Portland apartment, shivering and alone, wondering whether a window was open. He reached across the bed and found no warmth there, either. He thought that perhaps she'd ditched him, but then heard a cough from the living room and slid out of bed. A chill rose from the hardwood into the balls of his feet. He cracked the bedroom door.

Drapes waved in the December breeze. Aubrey was in the living room, sleeping on the couch, which she'd spun lengthwise and shoved partway through the double doors to the deck, her head resting in the open air.

~

Aubrey thumbed the straps of her backpack and looked around. "We should probably decide where to camp."

"Why not here?" The ground was covered in cushy brown layers of dried fir. There were dozens of dry, flat lots spread between huckleberry groves and evergreen trunks. To him it felt almost cozy.

"Let's find a spot on the beachhead by our kayaks."

"We're protected from the weather here. We won't even have to use the tent."

"It's dripping." She slapped her elbow. "And mosquitoes."

"What if a storm sets in overnight?"

She scratched her elbow and scanned the forested

roof. Wind hustled through its branches, and the leaves murmured.

~

Evening neared. The rain had stopped. The air smelled of wet soil. They hiked a few hundred yards from camp to the southwestern shore to catch the sunset. Aubrey set up a collapsible easel with one of the small canvases she'd brought along.

The forest grew thick and burly to the edge of the shoreline; past winter storms had created a shelf of rock and exposed roots dropping a dozen feet to the sea. Resting in a dark blue inlet a few miles away was a cabin cruiser anchored near another small island.

She pointed to the boat. "That's my focal point. It will be a nice lonely piece."

"Lonely?"

She leaned over, dug through her backpack, and pulled out a clear plastic bag filled with metallic tubes of paint. "Ever stop worrying?"

"I could ask the same thing." She was in her late thirties and wanted kids. After two months of dating, she'd asked him straight up if he intended on marrying and starting a family within the next couple years. They'd gone ring shopping. The ring she'd chosen was at that very moment snug in the interior pocket of his backpack. He'd had it now for three months. Time was ticking, but her past concerned him.

Aubrey stopped organizing the paint tubes. "What's up?"

"Nothing. Just thinking." He scanned the water and

rocked back on his heels. She looked distracted. It wasn't a good time to talk. She wanted to be left alone to paint. "I'm going to try to find a beach."

She smiled and returned to setting up.

He hiked away along the forest's edge. Though he fought it, his imagination never stopped wandering unlit hallways and picturing peanut butter and jelly sandwiches slid under shut doors. He didn't want to annoy her by prying. Was it prying? When you were talking marriage? Kids? Secrets between loved ones were perishable; if they remained hidden, their rot might spread.

At the same time, it didn't feel as though he had any right to force her to dwell in the trauma of her past. His gut told him that the right thing to do was to respect her privacy and pain. It was callous and uncaring to demand that she share it with him, but there was this one problem: you didn't get to choose who you fell in love with, but you did get to choose who you married.

~

A few months back, they'd visited her childhood home in Bend. In her room, he found her bed lying flush with the bay windows, as expected. Her paintings were Realist scenes from the nearby Cascade Mountains: Three Sisters, Bachelor, Tumalo, Broken Top, Three-Finger Jack. Evergreens, snow, alpine lakes, wildflowers. But in nearly every landscape, often tucked into the corner, stood the burnt shell of a house or some other broken-down dwelling. In the ones from early childhood, she'd signed her name on the bottom right corner: Beth Theroux.

When he'd thumbed through her yearbooks, he

discovered that between elementary school and junior high, she'd changed her name. A quick search of her friends' tributes revealed little more than variations of "Stay cool, don't change."

When he'd asked her about the cabins, she'd said something about juxtaposing the enduring qualities of nature with the impermanence of human structures. When he'd challenged the name change, she'd dismissed it as the simple vanity of wanting to be called something more sophisticated than Beth.

~

Owen found a thin, carved-out section of the forest edge near a lone swatch of beach. He took off his shoes and shirt and waded into the water. It felt warm; the sun must have baked the rocks and sand before the tidewater rushed in and smothered it. He looked down the shore and could see Aubrey up on the point behind her easel, crowded in by tan Madronas growing wild and distorted from the sea winds. She reached up and shook out her long, curly mess of hair.

He caught his breath. Lately, whenever he felt that clench of desire come upon him, it immediately turned to dull ache as he imagined what might have happened to her. He wished he could share that sorrow with her. That wish flickered to anger; she was hoarding it and pushing him away in the process.

He wondered whether he was just afraid of commitment and if he simply felt threatened by her silence because of it. He gazed at the sun shining over the outlying islands. The water was a mirror, and what blue it reflected would have felt inviting to most anyone else.

He glanced up. Aubrey waved. He waded further into the lagoon—he felt like he had to, if only to prove that he wasn't afraid. The cool water rose above his thighs. His breath quickened. There didn't seem to be much current. He kept on. The water met his belly button, then his midsection. He counted to three and made a half-hearted dive. The chill shocked his chest and his neck. He began to swim, first a couple of strokes, then a few more.

But when he tried to touch bottom, he felt only the formlessness of water. He turned, struggling for breath, feeling he might float away. The currents. He paddled as hard as he could toward shore, trying to keep his head above water. His lungs wouldn't fill. There wasn't enough air in the world.

He was about to call out to Aubrey for help when his foot scuffed the bottom. He surged forward until he was standing again, saltwater lapping at his stomach.

He turned and looked, panting. Again, Aubrey waved. Perhaps laughed. He couldn't tell.

~

Later that night, they were side-by-side in their sleeping bags, leaning against a downed fir. She'd fallen asleep after a dinner of freeze-dried linguine with fresh oysters from the beach.

An enormous owl swooped by the fire, grazing just over their heads, so low that Owen could see its serrated feathers and the stripes that marched out to the tips of its wings. He nearly screamed. His heart thundered. It was incredible how little sound its flight produced. It made him uneasy to imagine that it had been up there in the treetops, secretly watching, perhaps this entire time.

He turned on his flashlight and began casing the branches.

~

After he'd seen the paintings from her childhood home in Bend, he'd searched the web for Beth Theroux and found nothing. High school, junior high, still nothing. But a search for her elementary school produced a few archived articles talking about three unnamed children who'd been kidnapped and taken to a small cabin in the wilderness accessible only by dirt roads. The children were found within a week. The kidnapper's driver's license photo revealed little save a severe crewcut and eyeglasses with thick frames. He was apparently convinced that the world was on the verge of some apocalyptic event. He claimed he had enough stores to save three children and himself.

Owen tried to find out more information, but there was surprisingly little. After scouring caches of microfilm, he called the local paper, pretending he was a professor at Portland State working on a paper discussing ties between religious beliefs and kidnappings. The best he got was the number of the lead detective on the case. When he inquired about the identity of the kids and whether any abuse had happened, the detective got defensive. He wasn't at liberty to share that information. These were young kids, now grown. It was theirs to share, not his.

Owen printed out the clippings and showed Aubrey. Played it off like he'd been researching the best schools around Bend, just in case they moved to be closer to her family if-and-when they had kids.

At first, she didn't seem to remember. Then, eyes locked on the pages, she said, "Wait, yes, this rings a bell...at least I think it does. Poor girls. Thank God they were safe."

It was something someone would remember. Something *everyone* would remember. It was also the sort of thing that, if it happened to you, you might rather forget. The sort of thing that, years later, when faced with it directly, might cause you to rub your nose and shrug and not make eye contact with the person who was asking, even if you loved that person, even if that person loved you. And she'd said "poor girls;" the article hadn't mentioned gender.

~

Owen was nearly asleep when a scattering of creaks distracted him. He sat up. He couldn't feel the wind—only hear evidence of its busyness above.

Aubrey began to stir. Then she tensed up, startled, and shook loose her arms. She pushed up onto her knees. Her eyes were sharp. "Where are we?"

"It's just me." He tried to grab her hand, but she shoved it away. "It's me, Owen. We're camping. On an island in the San Juans."

"I can't sleep here." She began unwrapping herself from her sleeping bag.

"We're perfectly safe."

"I want to sleep on shore."

"It's fine."

"Whatever." She turned on her flashlight and began scanning the ground until she found her sandals.

"Wait. Let's talk about this."

"Nothing to talk about." She corralled the sleeping bag into her arms.

"Why won't you tell me what's wrong?" It was out before he could stop himself. He stood up. "The thing is, I feel like—"

"Yes, I know." She grabbed the bag tighter. "You feel like I'm hiding something. And you won't let it go."

"It's just—"

"I love you, but I'm starting to wonder what this is really about."

The fire popped, and there was a rustling from the trees overhead.

"I just don't like secrets," he said.

She took a deep breath. The fire lit her eyes. "I'm not sure what you want me to say."

He took a step towards her. "I just wish we could talk. Especially about the stuff we don't want to."

"And?"

"Okay. Fine. Were you one of those girls?"

"There it is." She shook her head. "Look. I need to know that you're okay with me."

"Of course, I'm okay. That's the whole reason we're having this conversation."

She scoffed and turned and began walking. Her sleeping bag dangled from her arms and crinkled as it slid along the ground behind her. "I'm not going to be some project," she said over her shoulder. "Some mystery for you to solve."

"But I love you—" She stopped. "Don't you trust me?"

"How can you even begin to talk about trust when you won't talk to me about—"

She turned and left.

~

Owen circled the fire, kicking dirt over the gasping embers. He gathered his sleeping bag and walked through the still forest until the breeze began fingering in from between the trunks. Farther along, faint moonlight started to peek through the tree line, and soon he could hear gusts of wind rushing up against the island.

He shut off his flashlight once he reached the edge of the forest. He spotted Aubrey lying sideways near the tide line. He laid out his sleeping bag behind her.

She pulled tight into her own bag and sniffed.

"I'm sorry," he said.

She didn't reply, but turned over and looked at him, face puffy and wet with tears.

He pressed his hand into her shoulder. She trembled, and it occurred to him that her misery granted him relief. He dismissed the thought and looked out at the ocean. The wind had died down, but he could still hear the dark waves crashing on shore.

"Come here," she said.

He hesitated.

"Let me." She reached out. "Please."

He shivered and lay down beside her. She closed her eyes and rested into his neck.

Beyond were the wide-open sky and the sea. He couldn't fathom why they comforted her. The wind would pick up, and it would probably rain, and by morning they would be soaked. And that same cabin cruiser, still anchored in the inlet, lights beaconing in the dark; what was going on inside that cabin? He would probably never know. Just like he would never know what she imagined was going on inside the cabin.

He could handle that, he decided. He would handle it. He reached into his pocket for the ring. He took her hand and pressed it into her palm. "Will you?"

She lifted up and studied his face. She laughed and kissed him hard.

Beyond, out in the channel, the deck lights of the cabin cruiser flashed. Its engine turned over a few times, but struggled to catch.

Lap Lane

I tried to explain to Sammy that seventy percent of beach drownings occurred within ten yards of a person who could help.

"Seems made up," she said. The bottom of her chin looked turquoise from the reflection of the water.

"No, it's true. I read it somewhere legitimate. I remember thinking, *This is actually true.*"

A scene of two women kick boarding side-by-side during adult swim probably sounds like it should be on the front cover of an AARP leaflet, but we liked the fact that we could get a low-impact workout and still talk the whole time. And I guess we weren't really that young anymore.

"So what do you mean by 'the family was around,'" she asked.

"That's the thing. They were playing in the surf right next to him."

"What?!"

Sammy had almost shouted. The echo of her voice slapped off the tile walls and the water. When I met her during our freshman year of college, she was a cheerleader. Being loud was nothing for her.

"I know," I said. "It's wild to think about."

"They were there? That sounds...I don't know how that sounds."

I imagined she was thinking the same thing I was, that it sounded unthinkably sad. We kicked for a while in silence. I caught a strong scent of chlorine coming off the adjacent hot tub where an older guy with an artificial tan and nose plugs was climbing in. I was thankful that the whirlpool jets provided some white noise. Voices carry over water.

"Was a lifeguard around?" she asked. "God. If one was, save another spot under the bus."

These were my neighbors we were talking about, the family in the story. "I don't think anyone deserves to be under the bus."

"Well, it would be one thing if the kid ran away and you couldn't find him and then he drowned."

"How is that different? It's not like they intended—"

"They were right there," she said.

We reached the end of the pool, so we turned around and pushed off the side and continued kicking.

She said, "I have two kids. Sometimes they run off and things can happen. You can't control everything. But if you're there? It just seems like a whole other level."

"It's so tragic."

"And that," she said.

We kicked for a while in silence and talked about people we both knew, things that had happened to them, things they did. Then, for some reason, I told her something I'd never told anyone. I just felt like I had to say it, and she was there, so I told her how, when I got home from work most nights, Tom's eyes already had that glossy film over them. How I appreciated that he pretended not to be drunk and asked me questions about my day, but then he sometimes ended up asking the same questions twice in the same conversation without realizing it. It was like he was there one minute, then gone the next. This was most nights.

Sammy didn't say anything. She kept looking straight ahead, kicking. Finally, she said, "I don't know what to say."

There were still fifteen minutes left of adult swim.

I said, "So tell me about Timothy. He's starting Kindergarten next fall, right?" The conversation continued from there.

When I got home, I found that article I'd read. It was on the American Lifeguard Association website. I forwarded the link to Sammy. I was right; once your air supply gets below a certain level, your basic bodily functions take over, and the only thing you can do is attempt to breathe. It can look like someone swimming next to you is fine when, in reality, they are unable to say a word or stop themselves from dropping below the waves.

Switchback

Down the dry path through the firs and moss and vines and bustles of mountain blueberries the innocent ran. He knew he wasn't fast enough to escape, but he believed in miracles, so he continued on, if only to allow more time for God to work. The sound of the men from the camp chasing him had grown louder over the last quarter mile. All that mattered was that the tiny cloth sleeve he'd stolen lay safely inside the pocket of his thin, woolen trousers—a sleeve filled with small, kernel-like seeds, so few, so small, by appearance little more than sand, seeds that would heal the world, the prophet had said. The theft was the only physical sin he had knowingly committed, though violence often played in his young mind. For this reason, he feared the men; he'd not only heard stories of them, but he'd imagined in great detail what they might do if they caught up to him. He crossed himself.

At a switchback near a small alpine pond, his endurance failed. He heard the barks of dogs—they would likely be the first to catch him. Winded, he stopped, leaning over, coughing, praying. Morning sun shone across the path: canary, butter, butterscotch. He removed the seed sleeve from his trouser pocket. He considered dumping them out and hoping they'd grow, but he didn't have time to bury them, and the ground was a leaf, warped brittle by the changing of seasons. Thinking of nowhere to hide them, he poured the seeds into his dry mouth, conjuring enough spit to make a paste to store under his tongue. He threw the empty sleeve into the bramble on the side of the path just before the dogs and the men rounded the switchback. They stopped, and some began mocking him, perhaps in delight at what would soon follow. They looked haggard, all of them, even while they were triumphant. Did he have the seeds? Would he tell where they'd gone? No.

These are my people, he thought, as a chestnut-bearded man gripped his arm tightly enough to make him wince. *These men,* he thought, *they know not what they do*. He exhaled a last, brief breath of fear, and his heart settled. He no longer cared what they did to him. He cared only about the seeds in his mouth, resting against his gums. His time wasn't yet spent. As the prophet once said, "The logic of miracles is the wisdom of fools."

Jeering at him, leering, they walked together to a sun-torched meadow, tan as the gut side of an uncured belt. The stout, bearded man struck him. As he fell, he could hear the rest of the men cheer. Then, at the orders of the bearded man, two of the others tied his hands and ankles and carried him toward the soft, damp soil near the creek feeding the pond.

The two who carried him began digging a grave. Head sideways on the ground, he watched and was met with the sort of inspiration that only the arrival of death can bring. It occurred to him he'd been caught up in a miracle. They would bury him, but in his mouth were the seeds. Next to the creek, the seeds would grow, wrapping their roots through his tongue and throat and face and body, nourished by the damp soil surrounding him. He was lowered into the grave, ankles and wrists raw, and he blessed the men, each of them, as they laughed over his words. Laughed. Laughed as if their souls weren't in peril for the very miracle they were helping to perform.

It's Like This

I'm tired of the old drunk next door trudging up the steps to my home at inappropriate times like seven in the morning and ten at night to comment on the tire pressure of my Toyota and ask how the kids are doing even though I've told him a dozen times they live with their mother now. It's none of his business. He's just an old, lonely drunk who's fucked up his life and thinks he's found a kindred spirit or something. I caught him one time opening the lid to my recycling bin and peering in as if to check out what I'm drinking. Again, none of his business. I should have said something—right then, yelled out the window—but he's so old, I didn't want him to dust out on my watch. Anyways, as I was saying, it's like this: he's the itchy burr under the collar of that old Christmas sweater that used to fit before I gained all that weight. This is the guy. Big. Fat. Drunken. Burr. I know, maybe I'm being too hard on him. It's really not so bad. This world, you know. We're just crowded together like mussels on a pier block, waiting for the tide—that's what I told my daughter just last week. But what I'm saying is this: every night, I watch him there through the window, drinking through another sitcom, and sometimes I can even see the show he's watching, and it's the same show I'm watching, and it just pisses me the fuck off. Don't ask me why I care so much. I don't even feel bad for the guy. Like I said, it's his own life he fucked up. But if you saw him, you'd get what I'm saying. You can even smell it. It's true. Sometimes when I'm watching, it's like I can smell his sour breath in my fucking beer.

Fit to Scale

Even at age eleven, in its infancy, it was there—the slight narrowing of vision, the increased glare of the lights, the moment of dizziness. At that time, I called it déjà vu because that was the closest description I'd heard. The feeling hit me as I strolled through the stacks of floor-to-ceiling model kits, pressing in from all sides of the narrow aisles of the hobby shop. There was no discernable order to the stacks, just a huge mess, each box stamped with glossy photographs or illustrations of what willing hands could build. Tanks, fighter jets, biplanes, aircraft carriers, jeeps—military models from every war, accurate down to the decals. This was Seattle in the winter of 1991, and the chaos in the hobby shop was both glorious and unnerving. It seemed as if anything could be hiding in there. That was both the problem and the reason for my coming. I was searching, but for what, I didn't know.

My friend Cy jimmied a box from the middle of a tall stack, careful not to send any other models tumbling. I noticed the skin of his arm had faded to rich butter from its summertime darkness. I was jealous of his skin, if jealousy included the desire to touch. My own skin had three colors: the dark orange of freckles, the burgundy of sunburns and embarrassment, and the pallor of the spaces between. Cy's, on the other hand, was elegant, regardless of the season.

"P-51 Mustang," he said of the box, still awed, even though I'd watched him handle that model at least a dozen times before. It was an import from France, more expensive than the American models. The foreign ones were difficult to make, thus more desirable. For some, you only had the visual directions to follow.

Ron, one of the owners of the store, walked down the aisle and plucked the box from Cy's hands. He flipped it around, causing the plastic sheets inside to clack. "This one bites," he said. The rendering of the fatigue-green WWII fighter plane on the front of the box portrayed a lifelike set of predator's teeth below the cockpit. Cy wanted the model more than me, but I pretended otherwise because that was the way of friendship.

Mitch, the shop's co-owner, hollered from his usual spot behind the register in the front of the store. "What are you saying to those boys about biting?"

Ron's laugh ended with a propane hiss. He sported a large beard that didn't hide his double chin so much as dress it up. I liked him, but felt ambivalent toward Mitch, who was tall and skinny and never without one of those small-rimmed cycling caps. Mitch didn't pay much attention to the customers, only to Ron, and when forced to talk to one of us, he always found a way to corral his partner back into the conversation.

My mother had warned me about Ron and Mitch. "You know they're queer, right?" she asked. "Try not to spend too much time there." I knew what she meant by queer, but didn't want to believe her, not about them. I'd only ever heard of someone's cousin's sister who'd had it happen to them, but even that was only rumors from somewhere else. Not around here. Not at the hobby shop.

Ron retreated to the register. Cy and I perused the models, but after a few moments, Ron interrupted us again. He peered at me through thick glasses that magnified his eyeballs to the size of plum pits. "David," he said. "I want you to tell your mother something for me." His breath smelled of Top Ramen. "Tell her we hope she reconsiders. She'll know what I'm talking about."

~

Later, I walked through the door of my mother's empty beauty salon and relayed Ron's message. "What does he mean?" I asked.

My mother set her broom against the wall. Her salon was in the same strip of shops bordering the outdoor mall, only half-a-dozen doors down from the hobby shop. Next to the shop window sat a couch, a few chairs, a small television set, and a bunch of magazines gathered on the side tables adjacent to helmeted dryers. Photos of outdated hair models lined the walls. In the center of the shop were two baby blue leather swivel chairs, one of which my aunt Liz used until a year ago when she moved to Walla Walla to open a shop of her own. The chair had remained empty since her departure.

"Did he tell you anything else?" my mother asked.

"No."

She muttered to herself and slapped her hand on the seat of one of the big cushioned chairs. This was strange because I never got to sit in her swivel chairs, just in case someone drove by and decided not to come in because they assumed she was helping a customer. I hopped up and felt the soft leather depress beneath me.

"Here's the thing…" She told me that the ownership of the outdoor mall had changed, and they were raising rent and removing the ban on chain stores, effectively forcing nearly all the shops—which were already just getting by—

to either pony up or get out. "So Ron and Mitch want to form a group to sue the new management for breach of contract. They're allowed to raise rent, but letting in the chains is another matter. We'd never compete."

One of the reasons for Aunt Liz's departure was the rent in her apartment complex doubling over the last few years. The area around the mall had been changing. Cranes had begun appearing on the horizon, there to build huge condominium structures, and now broad, upscale houses peppered neighborhoods that hadn't seen any new architecture in decades.

"How long before it gets figured out?" I asked, assuming mom was going to join the fight along with Ron and Mitch. In every story I'd ever heard, when something painful occurred, good people fought back and won.

She put her hands on her hips. "Ron and Mitch are fools. It's just a matter of time before they go out of business. And I'm not going to waste a bunch of money on some lawsuit. If we did actually end up winning, there'd still be a hundred other ways the new management could sink us."

A sedan pulled into the parking lot. She shoved me off the seat, but the car drove past. My mother crossed her arms. The look on her face spelled guilt. "Look, David. I can't afford to be noble here. I have you and your father to think about."

"Why won't you fight?" I didn't say the word *coward*, but it was on my tongue. "What does Dad say?"

She ignored my questions and told me that I should prepare myself for the possibility of moving that summer, following Aunt Liz to Walla Walla. She began to explain how it all might work, but I was no longer paying attention. It felt ridiculous. We weren't moving. No way. Outside, snow had begun to accumulate in the empty parking lot. With luck, school would be canceled, and tomorrow we'd be sledding, and that was that.

~

That night, General Schwarzkopf appeared on television with a long steel pointer and megaton jowls. "This is Desert Storm," he said, while an officer helped him through a series of tag boards loaded with graphs and figures and maps detailing the campaign.

"And so it begins," said my father, sitting next to us on the couch, polishing off the little compartment of corn in his Swedish meatballs TV dinner. "And who on God's green Earth knows when it will end?" He'd served in the Vietnam War. Like so many others, he was haunted both by his service and by the fact that he was haunted, truths I didn't recognize until too late. He was self-employed as a fix-it guy, but didn't work much. I never heard my parents talk about it, but it was always there, like the background hum of a refrigerator.

I ran to the telephone in the kitchen and dialed Cy. "Did you hear?"

"Finally," he said. "It's on."

Neither of us could wait to see what sorts of machinery and vehicles and planes the military would reveal. We'd never experienced anything other than the Cold War, and that meant we'd had to rely on the memories of others in terms of what full-fledged warfare was like. We wanted the real thing. Bared teeth. New fighter jets. New dogfights. And now it was happening.

The television aired endless clips of the nighttime cityscape streaked with anti-aircraft fire. Then they showed a daytime shot of a short, squat, matte black triangle that looked like a burnt slice of pizza with tail flaps. The Stealth Bomber. No one had seen anything like it. Nor could they, not even on radar, because it was invisible. How was that even possible? This new geometry was going to bomb the crap out of the Iraqis.

"It's disrespectful," said my mother to the television. "If it's truly invisible, how is that a fair fight?"

My father grabbed a beer from the sixer sitting next to him on the couch. He pushed on the tab until it coughed. "What's fair ever had to do with it?"

~

The next day, Cy and I hustled from school to the hobby shop. The bell above the door rang as we rushed to the stacks to see if any of the new models had arrived. As far as we could tell, there were only a few new aircraft carriers and a Korean-War-era B-29 Superfortress. We returned to the front of the shop.

"Where's the new models?" Cy asked.

Mitch, behind the counter, had a tiny brush in one hand and what looked like a miniature plastic cowboy in the other. He didn't glance up from his project. "Ask Ron."

"Where is he?"

"On break. Back in fifteen."

Cy stuffed his hands into his pockets, and we meandered back down the aisle. I dragged my fingers over the stacks of cardboard boxes. The shop smelled like hot glue and paint.

"Do you still want the Mustang?" I asked Cy.

"No," he said, as if the question was stupid. "It's lame."

"Yeah. Totally," I said, even though I couldn't have cared less. Cy was so certain of what he wanted, so comfortable with his desires.

He stopped and peered over my shoulder and then whispered. "You know who's lame?"

"Who?"

"Mitch and Ron. I heard they're butt buddies."

I laughed and felt my face color. "Yeah, right."

"Swear to God," he said. "My dad says so."

"How would he know?"

Cy blinked. "He's a cop."

Before I could respond, Ron bustled through the door and limped down the aisle towards us. He appeared to have injured his hip, but was trying to ignore the limp it caused. He rubbed his big hands together and smiled. "I only need one guess as to why you boys are here."

"What's that supposed to mean?" Cy asked. He was glaring.

Ron looked confused. I noticed that he had a dark circle beneath his left eye. It looked as though he may have tried to cover it up with makeup.

"What happened?" I asked.

He looked at Cy, then at me. "Nothing. I fell off my bike."

Cy began to snicker, and I felt like I should laugh along with him. That would have been the safe thing to do. But nothing about this struck me as funny.

"So when do the new models come in?" Cy asked.

Ron limped back towards the register. The shoe on his injured foot made a short sliding sound on the linoleum.

"They're backordered a few weeks," he said. "I'll lct you know."

Mitch coughed into his fist and shook his head, still not looking up.

~

They announced the end of the war just a few days after it had begun. Cy was over at our house for a slumber party, and we were waiting for my parents to finish with the news so we could watch a war movie we'd pooled our money to rent. On the news, grainy footage from high above showed missiles plummeting into smokestacks, pounding buildings to dust. Iraqi troops walked under the sun with their hands cupped over their heads, surrendering by the thousands. I remember being disappointed. Sure, we'd won, but it felt cheap. It was barely a fight.

"This is how they imagined 'Nam would go," said my father from the couch, an overturned potpie steaming on his plate, empty tin shell resting on the arm of the couch.

"Be happy," said my mother, stabbing at cubed carrots. "It's all but over."

My father scoffed. "A war can be all-but-over for an entire fucking decade before the last shot is fired."

"Dan," my mother said. "We have guests—"

"You think he's never heard the word fuck before?"

Cy laughed. She glared.

"Fine," he said, and picked up the potpie and left out the porch door towards the garage. This had been happening more often of late: my mother correcting, him leaving. I thought nothing of it then, what it must have felt for my father to feel out of line in his own house, how it must have felt for my mother to have to try and shield me from his descent.

My parents went to sleep around nine. Cy and I watched the war movie which contained far fewer battle scenes than the jacket cover promised. Once it was done, we turned out the lights and ruminated for a while in the dark over the various girls in our class and what was most attractive about them. Cy had a sister in high school who'd told him about her excursions with the opposite sex.

"We practice sometimes," he said, about him and his sister.

"What do you mean?"

"Like we practice making out. Let me show you."

He rolled over on top of me. I could feel his weight pressing into my pelvis through the sleeping bags. His breath smelled of the red licorice he'd just eaten, and his beautiful skin was closer to mine than it had ever been. I felt my heart in my cheeks and ears.

"You're supposed to open up your legs," he said.

I did, and he began driving his hips into mine. He was pretending I was Amy. When it was my turn, I pretended that I was pretending he was a girl named Crystal who I'd told him I thought was cute. We were playing, but it was the sort of play people never talked about, never admitted, not the next morning or even when grown, for fear that it had meant something, for fear that it might mean something. Only the flannel layering of our sleeping bags lay between us. I was filled with that sharp buzz I'd felt in the hobby shop, that dizziness, that brightening of senses. I could no more ignore my arousal and exhilaration than the panic that scorched it.

~

Winter dragged on, and the war became a conflict—a difference that seemed only semantic. My mother alluded to the potential move to Walla Walla, but I ignored her much in the same way I ignored what had happened that night with Cy. To an observer it might have seemed that everything returned to its usual rhythm. But I remember one day in particular, just before baseball season was to begin, when both Cy and I went into the hobby shop to check for any new arrivals. We scanned the boxes without any luck.

"I've saved up enough for the Mustang," Cy said. "But I still want the Stealth."

"I thought you said the Mustang was lame."

"You're lame," he said, and shook his head.

Ron was at the register, reading a magazine. Mitch was in the back, gluing a tree to a railroad feature he'd been working on for what seemed like forever. The scene was a beautiful take on the American high plains, though I never had the guts to reveal my admiration. Horses sipped from a clear blue pond, flanked by flannelled cowboys with miniature pistols in holsters around their belts. The train swerved in and out of tunnels and feigned a stop at a crowded depot outside of a town shadowed by mountains so tall the summer's heat couldn't melt the snow. It was the sort of place I yearned to live.

"Why aren't the new models here?" Cy asked.

"I ordered them months ago," Ron said. "I told you guys that you'll get first dibs once they come in. But I can't control when that is."

Cy rolled his eyes and stuck his hands in his pocket.

He strolled down the aisle toward the Estes rockets that we always talked about buying but could never quite bring ourselves to purchase.

I was about to follow him when Ron grabbed my shoulder. "Has your mother reconsidered?" His eye had healed, but I'd noticed he still walked with a slight limp.

I shrugged off his hand and felt a twinge of shame as I did so. "What do you mean?"

Mitch looked up from the models.

~

My mother told me what he meant that night, in front of the television where men with glossy hair discussed the lingering skirmishes in the Middle East and the need for continued military presence. "We're going," she said, arms crossed, defiant, after trying for a good half-hour to help me understand. My father munched a pizza bagel in silence. He'd already signed on with a service station in Walla Walla.

"No," I said. "We're not. The school year isn't even done."

My mother looked at my father.

He closed his eyes for a moment while chewing his bite, then looked at me. It struck me how tired he looked. The whites around his pupils had somehow dulled, and the pockets beneath were gray. "You should be happy," he said. "Your summer vacation is starting on Monday."

I ran to the kitchen and dialed up Cy on the phone. "Can I come over? I have something to tell you."

"Sorry man," he said. "My parents are out at some auction and my sister is out at a movie, so Amy is coming over. You'll have to give Ron a call."

He hung up before I could say anything. I slammed the phone into the receiver so hard the casing cracked.

~

I skipped school the next day, the first time I ever did so, but far from the last. It was strange, walking around the neighborhood knowing that it was no longer mine, realizing that this world I'd inhabited my entire life would be taken from me without my permission, without even a fight. A place can be so familiar but can become foreign in the span of a day.

There was nothing else to do, so I walked the three miles to the hobby shop. The sun burst through the clouds here and there, but not long enough for me to remove my parka.

I opened the door to the shop, and in one of those details that only become important because of context, the bell over the door failed to ring when I entered. Behind the counter, I saw Mitch seated on Ron's lap, arm around his neck, while Ron played with the buttons on Mitch's flannel. Both of them kissed each other gently in the way of two people in love.

Something inside me concussed. I ran down the aisle and began toppling all the stacks. These were models of war planes, fit with miniatures of bombs that killed, piloted by people who, years ago, took quick breaths as they soared over enemy territory, many on the way to their own deaths. Outside was a world where business deals were made by real people eliminating the jobs of others; where families moved because they had no other choice;

where fathers lost wars with themselves and fell asleep in garages with their cars still running; where men were applauded for accosting women but were feared and hated for kissing men. Where men were called faggots and all the other names they had for us, even if, growing up, we might have wished we were straight, if only because it was so damn easier.

Before Ron and Mitch could catch me, I ran out of the store into the parking lot and past my mother's empty salon, yearning to return to the world I'd inhabited before, not realizing that world no longer existed, not realizing how terrible and wonderful that was.

Libidonomics

I was sold on Liz Fletcher well before we sat down for Mexican food. She checked groceries at the Smith's by my primary residence in the foothills, and for the previous month I'd shopped there every day—sometimes twice— just to get a chance to talk to her. Let's just say that every time I saw her my aisles got stocked.

I'd asked her out a dozen times in jest until she finally said, "I'm off at five," if nothing else just to shut me up. Understand: I'm neither young nor attractive, but I'm persistent and have money. A man has to make do with what he's got.

When our margaritas arrived, I asked her what she would do if she could do anything she wanted in the world and not worry about money. I told her I didn't want to hear anything about world peace or planting trees for tomorrow. Those were fine, of course, but I wanted the secret desires, the selfish.

She blushed. "I've always wanted to be a model."

Of course she had. I imagine that, by age ten, most women have spent thousands of hours walking down imaginary runways and across fictional stages with cameras flashing in adoration, but by God, here was someone whose childhood dream had a chance of coming true.

I asked her, "What's stopping you?"

"What do you mean?"

She looked shocked that I'd taken her seriously, further proof of there being too many repressed snobs in the world making people feel bad for un-starched desires.

Naturally, I asked her if she'd entered any beauty contests, gotten any photos taken, or queried any agencies. After all, this wasn't the moon. We were only a forty-five-minute drive to downtown.

She shrugged and wiped sweat from the coupette glass with her finger. I'd shamed her. She was one of those beautiful girls who no one had ever taken seriously, someone folks assumed hid no depth when, in reality, she had hopes and dreams and feelings like everyone else. And here I was, pushing her to be something she'd never been allowed since she hit puberty: a normal human being.

As it would turn out, that conclusion wasn't just premature, but generous. I tend to imagine the best in people.

Anyhow, I apologized a couple of times until she made eye contact, and then asked her, dead serious, what kind of model she wanted to be—"C'mon, tell me"—and she took a long sip of margarita as if to re-bolster her confidence.

"Centerfold," she said. "Is that embarrassing?"

Her shoulder was bare and the light was proud to touch it. There is no shame in a nude human body, only glory. I wanted to make her dreams come true. I wanted her to never break eye contact with anyone again. "It's beautiful. Never be embarrassed by your dreams."

The waiter brought out an iron skillet full of beef and onion and pepper, still crackling and spitting. I worried our bare arms would get spot burns. Then and there, an epiphany blossomed.

"We can't eat yet," I said.

She nodded and folded her hands and bowed her head. She thought I meant we should pray first.

"No, darling," I said. "I've got something here. See,

they bring out the fajita skillet too hot to eat, so that while we're waiting, we get that sweet experience of having our food in front of us, enticing our senses, but with an aching two-minute delay before it cools down to where we can dive in. We want it even more because we can't have it yet."

She blinked.

"Anticipation," I said. "Compels mothers to give up their firstborn."

She looked confused and, granted, what I said had no point of reference. I explained that I was talking about modeling and her dream of being a centerfold. We needed to find a way to make her too hot to touch. We needed to photograph her in such a way that the anticipation would be so thick and steamy that her photograph would be irresistible to the powers that be.

"That's all we need to capture your dream," I said, and I began to improvise a loose plan to make her a star while she nibbled at the beef.

I got excited. I barely touched the fajita platter for the rest of the night. Her eyes were wide with what I took as awe.

~

Convincing Liz to quit her job and come live with me was more difficult than I expected, considering her alternate path of Vitamin D deficiency and tendonitis from spending her days as a checker at Smith's. Did I mention the medieval dump of a split-level she'd been living in with some outwardly-morose waif from the meat department and a Chili's waitress with acne to spare? I offered her the car of her choice, a healthy allowance, and a new wardrobe. She said it wasn't about that.

It started to make sense how Liz had gotten to where she was, both socio-economically and culturally. The world opens doors for beautiful women; by appearance, she should have been the rush chair at her sorority, on the fast track to a cush PR job downtown, if not doing the weather for a network affiliate. Not sharing leftover pizza with the skee-ball team from the local arcade. I painted her as the humble victim. Desire is blind, but it won't just blind you; it'll make you see things that aren't there.

Liz said that living and working together might not be a good idea, and I thought she was being careful not to move too fast. I told her we'd have plenty of personal space—she could have the whole east wing of the estate, and I'd never enter her territory unless she invited me over the intercom. My house is the largest in the county in terms of square footage, if you don't count sheds (and no one ever should, because, hell, what's next, counting dog runs? Chicken coops?). You get the point: my house is incredible, and I say that for no other reason than to let you know that Liz's situation was, shall we say, improved.

Look, it's not like I needed her to be impressed or even grateful. The last things I wanted to invite into our relationship were more power dynamics than there already were by virtue of our differences in age, beauty, and holdings, but it would have been nice if she at least recognized what I was doing for her, considering the lavish praise I gave for what she was bringing to the table (and, by the way, she ended up agreeing to take the allowance, car, and wardrobe, despite her misgivings).

Within the first week of our business meetings, we

decided our first play would be to get her entered into the Country Cuties competition in one of the more reputable of the sensual magazines, *Steam*. The competition was open to the public. Contestants submitted pictures of themselves, and a panel of judges—combined with the online votes of users—winnowed the competition from semis to finalists, and then to a champion. The winner got a cover, a spread, and a contract.

I did some market research and found that the track record of Country Cuties going on to modeling careers beyond that first contract was decent. Plus, I told Liz that since we were going the sensual route first, she wouldn't have to reveal the whole kit and caboodle. She'd get to make the rounds to the other sensual mags, do the swimsuit tour, and maybe even lock down a few films before showing it all. Naked didn't fit well with the fajita principle, at least not yet. The world hadn't even taken a smell.

Then I made my first mistake (other than the gracious assumptions regarding her character). It's funny how trouble always begins with virtue. I've always been proud of my discipline. I'm a routine guy, through and through. When Forbes did a web feature on my ethos—for anyone boring enough to care—I claimed discipline as the foundation of my success, so it was in my nature to believe that scheduling each of Liz's days would help her become more productive.

I should also say that the schedule was absurdly laid back. Pandering, in hindsight. We'd wake up and shower separately, smoke a bowl, and eat breakfast while watching Good Morning America, then work out in my fitness center. After that, she'd get free time for a few hours while I managed my fracking operations, after which we'd shower and meet up in the Jacuzzi and have a short little "howdy neighbor"—if you know what I mean— before a light lunch. We only engaged in business in the afternoons, and, even then, only until dinnertime. And most of that was research.

Sounds good, right? Liz hated it. She pouted from the moment I attached the schedule to the refrigerator. She thought I was trying to control her. 'Lock her down' were the words she used. Then, 'cage.' Cage! There were so many things I would have said if I didn't love her. That ninety-nine percent of the world would kill for such an imprisonment. That pride was the enemy of success until you'd achieved it. That if designer clothes didn't suit her, there was a vomit-green apron waiting for her at Smith's on some rusted-out hook next to the frozen Salisbury Steak Hungry Man meals that needed to be stocked.

I should have kicked her to the curb. Instead, I told her to remember the fajita. Remember the crackle! Remember your dream, my wildcat! You can do this. We can do this. "I know it's tough now, but it will all be worth it."

She took a deep breath, bit her painfully full lip, and finally relented, but consider the disagreement I just mentioned to be a foreshadowing of what was to come.

~

We stayed with this schedule for about a month with no real progress. We couldn't figure out how the fajita should look, and you only got to reveal a beauty like Liz Fletcher for the first time once. I wasn't about to have someone I was so dearly beginning to hate come off as trailer trash.

Then it came to me: the second epiphany. It was a Tuesday morning and already ninety degrees in the shade, so we skipped the hot tub and took a quick ride in the shallow end of the pool on an inflatable raft instead. Then we relaxed, and I went to the kitchen to get us iced tea and a joint from the humidor. When I came back out, Liz was still naked, but now in the middle of the pool on that same inflatable raft from our lunchtime screw.

And I saw it. Remember that old movie *The Graduate*? Northeast libs love that movie, and I knew for a fact that the ownership of *Steam* was littered with frat boys from Dartmouth, so I imagined a way to play off the famous scene with the oh-so-young-and-existential Dustin Hoffman by dressing Liz in a classic sixties bra and panties and then posing her on a lawn chair, bored, reading a magazine, sexy as hell—you guessed it—at the bottom of the pool.

It had the entire audience in mind. The simpletons would go for the skin, while the melancholies would get stiff from the subtext: she was drowning and didn't even know it, like we all are.

Well, once Liz realized I was serious about the shoot, she thought I was nuts. "How am I going to breathe?"

"We'll have a diver feeding you from an oxygen tank."

"That's not modeling," she said. "That's desperation."

I reminded her that quotidian definitions of beauty rarely captivated the hearts and minds of weary men. Take the *Seven Year Itch* and how something as strange as Marilyn Monroe calling the foul breeze from a Manhattan subway delicious—up through an iron grate, billowing her dress, "Oh here comes another one"—had aroused the complicated loins of generations. And when that wasn't enough, I reminded her of all that I'd done for her already and told her that, if she didn't like it, there was always a mop and aisle five (by that time I'd advanced in my weariness over her entitlement).

She agreed, but couldn't resist getting back at me for my little power play by informing me, that very night, over the intercom, that we would no longer be engaging in coitus, in order that she might better cultivate her sizzle.

~

Liz didn't warm up to *The Graduate* idea no matter how many times I tried to convince her. I'd learned by that point not to say anything, but I'd begun to question her resolve. It still never entered my mind that I might be getting played. I offered to get her coaches, dozens of them, for her posture, her gait, facial care, body toning, her diet. If she'd said the word, she could have had a full staff of experts attending her every bowel movement. But she treated my suggestions—I only recognize this now, of course—the way a prom queen from an 80s comedy might treat study skills advice from the hapless nerd who's going to end up doing her homework, regardless.

It's embarrassing to admit, but I'd become petrified of her leaving. I'd upped her allowance to the point that she was making six figures. She'd taken over driving my Maserati. No credit limit at Neiman Marcus. If she'd had the gall to ask me to sign over a stake in my mining empire, I might have agreed.

In the week leading up to the shoot, she developed a

glare that could freeze vodka. It both terrified me and made me feel more alive than I'd felt in years. People wonder why the rich so often make such stupid personal decisions, seemingly at odds with their careful business management. It's because they so rarely ever feel fear—real fear—and when they finally do, it's like a drug. You always want what you can't have, but when you can have pretty much everything, each elusive jewel—no matter how stupid and toxic—becomes irresistible.

I neglected my business responsibilities to try and make it work. I hired a scuba instructor to hang out with her on the bottom of the pool, as well as an ocean photographer and an aquarium light specialist. They all looked and acted like young Harrison Fords: always getting away with something, always up to no good, but softies at heart. I perceived nothing. Her dream was all that I thought about. If I made her dreams come true, she'd be happy, then we'd be happy, and finally I would have a love that loved me back.

I'm convinced that all three of those hires slept with her, in my house—perhaps in my bed, and perhaps all at the same time! The evidence was there: swimsuits, body hair, stains, but I ignored them, like so many lonely men before me.

My team and I realized that, while keeping the lawn chair situated on the bottom of the pool was easy, keeping Liz there wasn't. We'd failed to account for the fact that she had oxygen in her blood and lungs that was desperate to bring her body back to the surface. One of the makeup artist's friends had dealt with this sort of thing before, so we flew him out from Los Angeles, too.

In the end, we didn't need the makeup artist's friend

because the solution was something a monkey could've figured out. We zip tied the back of Liz's swimsuit to the lawn chair and got the photographs. And damned if they weren't hotter than a fajita from hell, which is to say that hell is precisely as advertised: easy to dismiss, but mighty difficult to resist.

Waiting for the results wasn't pleasant. I was so nervous I developed sores on the inside of my butt cheeks. I hadn't slept with Liz in over a month, and she was skipping out on our Blue Dream parties, too—probably to spend my money snacking with big leaguers like that stallion of a first basemen I watched taking a piss in my Juliet rose grove one morning (I said nothing). I took her to buy some dresses from Herve L. Leroux in France. She moped. I took her to Beacher's Madhouse to rub elbows with Hollywood's finest. She spent the night in the arms of a beached reality television star.

That didn't matter to me.

I'd placed all my hopes in her dream coming true. I figured, if it came true, she would love me, but the situation at *Steam* was dire. The online votes got Liz into the semifinals, but our artistry was losing out to more blunt, carnal photographic invitations to the strong-wristed readership. A little encouragement was needed for the tastemakers at *Steam*. I had my lawyer call them up and see if they required anything to help the process along, then sent over a bottle of Chivas Regal 50-year Royal Salute to each of them, along with boxes of Gurkha Black Dragons, just to make my intentions clear. It was a loss, as a class gesture always is to those with negligible taste. My lawyer talked to a host of plebes who were offended that I would try to mess around with their stupid contest. Finally, after I called in a favor from a client with arms dealer connections, we got someone on the phone with some fucking power. Now, you'd think the editor for a mid-level skin mag would exhibit a fair amount of moral flexibility, but he balked. He did say one thing that was helpful: "The only way she's getting on the cover is if you buy the damn magazine."

Call me a romantic, but if someone wanted me to make the cover so badly that they bought me a magazine to make it happen, I'd be pretty impressed. Maybe even touched.

Well, to tell Liz the news, I took her to dinner at the same restaurant we'd been in during the first epiphany.

"Liz," I told her, holding up a prickly pear margarita in a glass the size of a soup bowl. "Let's toast to you being not only the Country Cuties winner, but *Steam*'s new cover girl."

I watched as the color drained from her cheeks and filled those deceitful lips to smiling.

My heart almost stopped. She hadn't smiled at me in months.

"Don't fuck with me," she said.

"We've got a conference call tomorrow with the new editor."

I'll be damned if a perfect little tear shaped just like Aphrodite's rear didn't slide from one of her eyes, and I'd be lying if I denied that a tear in the shape of Hephaestus's stone heart didn't fall from mine.

"And Liz," I said. "It's only going up from here, because you're looking at the new owner of *Steam* magazine."

She was just about to give me a toast, but then

stopped, glass mid-air. A little of the margarita spilled onto the table in between us. "What?" she asked.

"You can call me Mr. Publisher."

She set her margarita down. The tears dried up, and a scowl wrecked her beautiful face. "So you're saying the only reason I won the contest is because you bought the magazine?"

I tried to explain to her how this all works, how these contests, these magazines, these awards, none of them are fair; it's all business, all buying and selling and who wants it bad enough. Dollars make these things happen. I told her that, if it wasn't me, it would be someone else. "This is proof of my love," I told her. Publishing? There isn't a worse investment. I was doing this for her. And hadn't her dream come true?

"You think you can buy me?" she asked.

"No, Liz, I'd never think that. These are just gifts. This is how I show my love." I could have shown it in so many other ways—God knows I tried—but she wouldn't let me.

She yelled at me. Told me all of the things she'd probably been telling all of the other visitors at my place since I'd first invited her in. I'd destroyed her dream, apparently. She called me a dream hog, said she didn't ever want to model again, said she'd have been better off just staying at the grocery store. "You can't buy Liz Fletcher," she said.

The fajita plate arrived, and there it sat in front of us, hot and sizzling. We just stared until it went quiet.

She moved to Los Angeles with the boys. You've seen her. She's spent time on all our screens. Can't help but see her, and deservedly so. But apparently I'm foul for recognizing it, and evil for helping her along.

Love someone. Really love them. Try to make their dreams come true. Give everything. Save nothing for yourself. See what happens.

What Happens

I'll give her this: the black lipstick really enhances her sneer, but it's all the further she'll go, the sneer, at least this time. If I didn't have something she wanted—the keys to the Civic—she'd make it a hat trick by giving me the finger and yelling *Fuck you!,* but nothing she can do will convince me to let her drive to God-knows-where accompanied by random, poor-intentioned guys without providing me locations, names, periodic texts, and a solid curfew.

"Why do you even care?" she asks.

"I always care."

"But I'm seventeen."

"Doesn't matter. You're still my daughter."

"So? You're my dad, and I don't need to know everything about you." She sets her hands on her hips. "You just don't trust me. For no reason."

Recognize this conversation? Most people lucky enough to have had parents that gave a shit took part in some form of it dozens of times.

She's wrong, though. This has nothing to do with trust. This has to do with the fact that I can't concentrate when I don't know where she is. It's a lifestyle issue for me because the big problem here is that I love her, and ever since she was born, her existence has made me very, very afraid that something might happen to her. But explaining that has never worked—she can't see it, not yet. So I flip it on her, tell her something that happened before she was born, something I know she'll think is unfair and manipulative. And she'll be right—what happens in life is often unfair and manipulates everyone and everything.

A year before she was born, I tell her, I found my father dead on a white plastic chair in the middle of his back lawn overlooking Puget Sound. His mouth was open just slightly, making it look as though he didn't care at all that the rain had scattered what little hair he had left, revealing too much of his freckled scalp, or that his sopping wet flannel shirt sagged over his belly, revealing too much of his yellow chest.

I tell her that beside him sat an empty coffee mug smelling of orange juice and rainwater and, in his pocket, hid an empty plastic bottle of the Percocet he'd been taking for his hips. Also in his pocket was a note that was too damp to open; I had to wait for it to dry before I could read it. The note contained a list of instructions detailing what to do with probate, as well as the locations of the keys and access codes for the lockboxes, safes, and bank accounts. But it said nothing at all about the decision itself.

Nothing.

As I speak, she stands there, black lipstick helping her show how cruel I am to tell her such a thing. A bastard.

And maybe she's right.

I told her the story to illustrate how a moment like that would change a person's entire outlook on life and instill in them not only a deep-seeded fear of losing those they love but also the need for those loved ones to provide locations and names, check-in often, and adhere to curfews. I was trying to coax some empathy from her so I might more easily obtain the information that would allow me to thrive for the next six hours. But if I'm a bastard, it's because I made a few parts of the story up. It was the gardener who found my father initially, and it hadn't rained, and the note was far from empty—in truth, it was more of a novella illustrating a whole mess of reasons why he killed himself. But none of those facts would help deliver the message I needed to get across.

And it did get across. I know this because now that I'm done talking, she just stands there, no sneer, arms crossed, motionless by the door, not knowing quite what to do. But she gets the point. I can tell. And I'm not surprised. She's a sharp young woman. My guess is she hasn't said anything because she's trying to figure out how she can still be indignant after what I've just told her.

For a millisecond, I spot what I think is suspicion pinching her penciled brows, and I think she might call bullshit on the story. As I said, my daughter is sharp. But some of what I've just told her confirms what she's already heard about her grandfather. There's enough truth to it that she won't take the risk.

And she doesn't. But I know soon she'll find a way to continue the argument, a way to be pissed, probably inside of a minute. She's too much like me.

As she watches me, I feel something happening in my stomach, the kind of discomfort that usually comes when I'm not being as straightforward as I could be—perhaps should be—with a person. I can see how it might seem unethical, even cruel, to invent extra details about an already tragic event to make it more powerful so I can get what I want. But the truth, what I know for sure, what I've already tried to tell her before—multiple times—is something that she can't understand and will never spark her empathy.

It's this: I know that teenage boys are always an inch

away from indiscretion. And the boys she hangs out with? What can I say? I don't trust them. And while she's strong and willful, she's also seventeen and prone to giving boys the benefit of the doubt when they don't deserve it. I hear her talk on the phone with her girlfriends. These boys, these victims of suburban angst, they can do anything they want, and she'll psychologize about why they did this and that until it seems the punks are completely justified in their actions. "No wonder he's like that," she'll say. They could steal her car—which is actually my car—and she'd still find a way not just to forgive them, but love them for it.

I remember when I was sixteen, wearing a denim jacket loaded up with band buttons and some Robert Smith starter-set eye shadow and how I viewed women, even despite my bleeding heart. I was a dog. The only thing that interested me was finding a way. There was this one girl who I invited to see The Cure when they came to town. After the concert, we found ourselves in the back seat of my car going further than we should have. She didn't exactly say no, but she didn't exactly say yes, either. It's not something I'm proud of now, but it was something I bragged about then. You get the point: I know what teenage boys are like, I know what my daughter is like, and I know how easy it can be for boys to push things too far. And I know how convenient it is, afterward, for everyone involved to pretend nothing happened.

My daughter and I are silent together in the living room for an amount of time that is beginning to get uncomfortable, even for me. I rock back on my heels, trying to be patient, trying to give her a chance to respond to what happened. But in the end, I can't help forcing the issue.

"Address, or no keys. Names, or no keys. Phone on, or no keys. A call at ten, or no keys. Home by midnight, or no keys."

"Dad, c'mon."

"The truth, or no keys. That's final."

She cusses under her breath and pulls out her phone. "I'm texting you the address."

In his note, my father said he'd wished he'd told my sisters and I more, which was odd, because it seemed like he spent so much of his life telling too much. Our ears got so bruised that the last thing any of us wanted to do was hear another word. Yet he hated it when we talked. You could see it in how his face would scrunch up with pain just before he was about to interrupt us and finish the conversation himself—a move that remained his signature to the very end.

I get the keys from my pocket and toss them to my daughter.

She grabs them from the air.

I turn and walk away before she can beat me to it.

Togetherness

Dozens of kids on a playground, a mess of sound and color, all dangling from webbing, spinning, swinging, booting soccer balls into goals, sneezing into masks in the freshly-mowed field—everyone is in motion except for Owen's daughter, Isabel. He's worried. From a small hill adjacent to the playground, he watches her rest against a post of the parallel bars, alone, looking down at her hands, maybe resisting the urge to chew her nails, a habit she'd probably picked up from him during their long days together in isolation. Most of these kids Isabel hasn't seen in person since the pandemic started. She's just getting used to it all again. They all are.

He hears his name and turns. It's Derek, the father of one of the kids in Isabel's distance learning class the previous year. They bump fists. His short black hair has thinned since he last saw him, but, other than that, he seems pretty much the same, wearing a ubiquitous, gray Patagonia shirt with a blue-and-orange fish spanning the chest. Before they can do anything more than exchange greetings, they're joined by Meredith, Derek's partner. She wears a black t-shirt, screen printed with a large turquoise heart, and her thick blond hair is fastened in a low barrette, shaping her face like an oval frame. "Owen," she says. "I saw your lovely daughter. My she has grown."

"You're, like, the third person to tell me that. It's funny, you don't notice when you're with them all day, every day…"

"Every. Single. Day," she says.

"Lord help us," says Derek.

"Lord help them," she says.

Owen laughs and glances over to the playground. Isabel is playing with her braid, talking to a couple of other girls at the edge of the grass. She's acting naturally, and he feels relief. "So yeah, did you have a good experience online with Ms. Okafor? Isabel loved her."

"Ms. Okafor was great," said Derek. "Remarkable the way the teachers pivoted to online learning. But I still worry that the kids may be behind."

"We're all behind together," Meredith says. She takes a sip of iced coffee. "As to your question about distance learning, it went well, all things considered."

"How did Errol hold up through it all?"

She glances over to Derek, but he doesn't notice. "Well, we were really blessed to have a good pod to quarantine with. Good families; good kids. Kept the bubble tight. I feel kind of bad admitting we had one, because, you know...We just got scared he would fall behind, socially."

That they'd formed a pod surprises Owen. He'd assumed they were also in isolation as a family, like him. On Facebook, they'd posted pictures of marches, politics, equity issues—and he appreciated that—but ever since school buildings closed, there were no pictures of the kids together on social media, nor of the parents. "For some reason I didn't realize you—"

"We wanted to keep it quiet because, well, you know how it is. But then the kids get on the playground, and next thing you know, everyone knows what brand of toothpaste you use. So might as well confess it up front."

"Actually, we're all getting together at the beach after the picnic," says Derek. "You're welcome to come."

"Thanks, that's kind of you," Owen says, because he feels he must be polite. Out on the field, he sees his daughter; she's alone again, watching a soccer game from the sidelines, kids whirring around her. She's wearing sandals, and he wishes he had convinced her to wear tennis shoes so she could play. She played soccer as a second grader but said that she didn't want to continue with it this year, despite him trying to convince her otherwise.

"Yeah," says Meredith. "You really should come to the party. After the kids finished up school, we decided to meet back up as a pod once a month. But we're hoping to branch out and make it a community event."

"So how many people were in yours?"

As she speaks, she seems to open up. "Six families, nine kids total. Kids all met at our house. We cleared out the basement. Five days a week. Eight-to-five." She shakes her head, as if in disbelief.

"Wow. How did you manage all of the kids?"

"Well, we were blessed with a fantastic teacher. Just graduated from Seattle Pacific in elementary education and needed a job. The kids absolutely adored her."

"But she was really just a tutor," says Derek, hands out in assurance.

Meredith blinks. "Yes. Not a teacher. We have to be careful not to say 'teacher.' It sounds like we were running a private school or something. And, as you know, we're public all the way."

She and Derek continue to tell about the experience— game nights, slumber parties, boundaries, disagreements. A plane overhead banks towards Sea-Tac, but Owen isn't listening. He wonders how many other families in the school had ignored health regulations and issues of equity and quietly formed pods and hired teachers. He imagines hours upon hours of those kids being together, elbow to elbow, masks off, with someone whose sole purpose was to walk back and forth between them to help with their online activities. He thinks of nine kids, playing together in a backyard, learning to work out their differences, supervised by a person with a master's degree in caring for them. He realizes that, for some, the classroom size had shrunk to a perfect number.

Isabel would never have those experiences, more than a year's worth, ones he'd assumed they'd all tacitly agreed not to have. He feels incredibly foolish for assuming such a thing, and he can't take any satisfaction in some moral high ground their isolation has won them, because he knows if he'd been asked, he likely would have let Isabel join their pod. He'd even thought about seeking one out. In the end, he'd been afraid of her getting sick and, conscious of the unfairness of pods, he figured people like Meredith and Derek would look down on it. These were the parents of the kids she'd be friends with, and those relationships were important to maintain, because he knew parents had creative ways of encouraging their kids to play with some kids more than others.

"How about you?" Derek asks. "What were your arrangements with Isabel?"

It takes him a moment to respond. In his mind, he sees her sitting across the room from him, both in front of their computers, struggling through work. He recalls how, as the pandemic wore on, their free times together—breakfast, lunch breaks, late afternoons—were more and more filled with silence, and she began to ask to read in her room with the cats instead of going for a walk to the park with him.

"Are you okay?" Meredith asks.

"It was just the two of us."

"That's wonderful." Derek rubs his hands together. "I bet you guys grew close. That's special."

"So, so special," Meredith says. "Though I'm sure it was tough. I bet, in some ways, you'll look back at this time as a blessing in disguise. Well, like I said, we really hope you'll join our party. We have plenty of pizza for you and Isabel."

"Thank you." It's the last thing he wants to do—go to the party—but Isabel is still out on the field, alone. A group of kids nearby play what looks to be tag. He wills her to join in. She doesn't. "You know, let me get your phone numbers, just in case we can't make it. It would be great to get the kids together soon, either way."

After trading numbers, Derek and Meredith leave, and Owen finds some shade beneath a chestnut tree away from the rest of the parents. Isabel's still there by the soccer game, hands stuffed into the pockets of her shorts. He has a few conversations in his head where, instead of playing it casual, he calls out Meredith and Derek's hypocrisy, but his heart isn't in it because of Isabel. She's looking at her hands again, oblivious, as a soccer ball shoots past her, followed by kids chasing it, all rushing by her like salmon swimming upstream.

Glass

My neighbor wants to know about the fish tank, whether it still holds water. I want to know the same about the river running along the highway. There's a lot of agriculture upstream, a lot of fields to irrigate. It's midsummer, the sun is merciless, and the snowpack is gone.

He rubs his finger on the glass, looks at it, and wipes it against his jeans. I need more money than I can make from this yard sale, and I think he knows it.

"So what did you keep in the tank?" he asks.

"A better place than this." I kept tropical fish—a huge waste of money—but the tank was beautiful, and my job at the distributor didn't have an end date. I grew coral and had LED lights that made them glow. It drew your eyes from across the room.

He nods to the hose against the siding of the house. "Do you mind?"

"Be my guest." The man wears his jeans like a rancher, but his t-shirt is a size too large. The giveaway is his hair—it has the kind of sheen and lay that you can only pay for. He's playing local. He has land that gets the water from the river. I just know it. He heads over and turns on the water, then starts filling up the tank until it spills over the side. He could have believed me that the tank was fine, but I understand. A leak can appear from nowhere at any time, and before you can mend it, everything inside is gone.

He comes back, the tank dripping. "Checks out," he says. "You leaving town?"

"Greener pastures," I say. The things we all say are the

things that have all been said. Any conversation is confined to the form, like how a river may swirl and eddy, but it's always beholden to the bank.

"You and everyone." He nods to my cell phone in my hand. I'm waiting on calls for some jobs I applied to in the city. There's no job here that deserves me. I hope to never have to reconsider that comment.

"You know," he says, "I was talking to a guy at Albertson's the other day and he told me that if your cell phone drops in the water, all you need to do is put it in a bag of rice for an hour, and poof: all of the moisture is gone. That simple."

"I've heard that," I say, and it's true. I've heard it before a dozen times. What makes the fact surprising to people isn't that rice will soak up moisture—that's what rice does—it's that it will soak it up even from a piece of space-age technology.

"So what are you going to use it for?" I ask, nodding to the tank.

"A snake." He laughs. "I know. But once you capture it in glass, it's easier to believe it loves you back."

"It's a shame, isn't it?" I say, and he looks at me like he's lost. We're more alike than he's pretending we are. We're all alike. That's the problem. "I tell you what. How about you name your price and we'll go up from there."

The Keeper of Strays

Miles from town, miles from anyone's suspicion, Walter stood at the front window of his cabin, studying the evening's steep descent down the mountainside. The generator in the garage hummed through the wall. Earlier, he'd been out prepping his duck blind when a surprise, early-autumn snowstorm had forced him to shelter, knocking out power and phones in the process. Where before they were bare, the crags and boulders and bushes pocking the hillside now looked like knees and elbows pressed up into a massive white sheet. But Walter also spotted something red—or at least he thought he did—and not the burnt red of brittle fall leaves, but a painted red, a dyed red.

He rubbed his eyes and it was still there—bright. He pinched his fingers to his teeth and let fly a high-pitched whistle. Dozens of mutts—all of them strays he'd taken in—emerged from their resting places on couches, beneath beds, and clumped together in corners. They swarmed around his feet, huffing, whining, sneezing, wagging their tails, and dragging their bodies against the legs of his jeans.

He led them to the front door and swung it open. They rushed into the snow and hopped in and out of drifts down the hillside, resembling porpoises in the way they would sink and then emerge with arched backs.

A gust of wind threw flakes at Walter's face. He slammed shut the door, brushed the snow from his beard, and returned to the front window. The dogs carved intersecting lines through the snow. It didn't take them long to converge upon the swatch of red. They circled it and began to bay and howl.

Even from up at the top of the hill, behind the panes, Walter could see their snouts set high in the air, pointing back in his direction, calling their master to come and see what they had found and make judgment upon it.

Walter grabbed his shotgun.

~

By the time Walter reached them, the dogs had created a wide, circular swath of compacted snow around the object which lay under a large encasement of fresh powder. The dogs whined and sniffed and backed away and pointed with the joints above their paws.

With the butt of his shotgun, Walter brushed the snow from the swatch of cross-stitched red which he could now see was fabric. He brushed away more snow until a swipe revealed the blue of a bare fist.

He sucked in breath and set down the shotgun. No. No. No. He swatted wildly at the snow, revealing more of the body. He ripped off his gloves and felt the neck for a pulse.

"No!" he yelled. He stood up and circled the body. He kicked at the snow, kicked his shotgun, kicked at nothing. The dogs cowered from him, whining, until he sat down and began to moan and cry. Then they nuzzled his beard and forehead and licked the salty tears on his cheeks, and soon joined in on the howling. Were anyone around to hear, they might have feared for their lives, even though the sound represented the opposite of danger.

~

Once he made it back up the hill, Walter stopped beneath the awning of the door to his shed. The dogs slipped around his feet like river water around the stilts of a bridge. He followed them inside and found a wall to lean against. He was out of breath.

After he gathered himself, he ripped the dusty tarp from his snowmobile, straddled the seat, and flipped on the ignition. Nothing. He opened the hood, checked the gas and oil, then tried the ignition switch again. Nothing. He again popped the hood and fiddled with the mechanisms. The dogs milled around him, watching. A gust of wind whistled through the cracks in the shed, and, after a quick moment, left them again in the soft silence of snowfall.

Walter slammed shut the hood and wiped his brow with the back of his hand. He swore and left.

~

The strays made room for Walter as he dragged a burlap sack of dog food from the kitchen closet and let it come to rest beneath the overhead light in the middle of the kitchen. He pulled a steak knife from the maple block on the counter and made an incision through the center of the burlap sack. The dogs whined and sniffed the air and panted and dug their claws into the linoleum. Walter kicked the sack, and a few biscuits skittered onto the floor.

"This will be enough," he said. "Don't eat it all at

once." They came to him, and he knelt and scratched the soft spots behind their ears and let them nip his beard and clothes and hair.

"If you were a team of huskies, I'd take you with me," he said. "But it's too cold, and I couldn't feed all of you. And if I only took a few, the rest would never forgive me."

~

Back down the hill, the body was curled up, stiff from the cold or rigor mortis or both. Snow fell heavy as Walter lifted the body onto the yellow tarp that he'd laid flat on the circle of trampled snow. He wrapped the body in the tarp as one might swaddle a child.

"Your identification says your name is Anne," he said. "I'm Walter."

He stood up and saw that he'd wrapped the body poorly, all loose ends.

"There isn't a guidebook for this," he said to the body. "Something's wrong with my snowmobile. And there's no way my pickup could make it through to town. And who knows how long this weather will continue. We've no power, and no news. Everything's down."

He lifted the tarp-wrapped body onto a flat-bottomed sled he'd retrieved from the garage. He took a coil of rope from his pack and cut a few yards, then haphazardly tied the body to the sled. He cut another few yards of rope, made a loop, and attached both ends to the front of the sled. Then he stuffed the rest of the coil into his pack.

"I never had any children," he said. "But I have a strong imagination. I imagine you have parents, and that they are in a special kind of hell. They need to know about this now, not later. I imagine you would have wanted it that way. I imagine you might be watching this as we speak."

He tightened the straps of the snowshoe webs to his boots and shouldered his pack. He looked back at the house. In between the gusts of wind, barks from up the hill called out.

He stepped into the loop of the rope and lifted it up until it found a snug place on his belly just above his belt.

~

A few hours later, up ahead in the dusky lume of snow, a mute gray disc appeared: the lake. Walter wiped sweat from his eyebrows and continued along the buried path through snow-dusted evergreens. The dead body, covered by the tarp and tied fast, scraped along behind him.

"I'm going to need to stop, Anne. I need a rest. There's an overhang up the path here."

A dozen yards ahead, the overhang yawned. Walter moved toward it, brushing aside the blueberry bushes and huckleberry brambles crowding the path along the shoreline flats. Many of the leaves were still green, and some of the branches still clutched ripe berries, unprepared for the cold and just as surprised as everything else by the storm.

Walter put his gloves to his lips and yelled some loud nonsense. No wild animals scattered from beneath the overhang. There was no sound at all.

"Welcome to the Marriott," he said.

He dragged the sled inside and sat down. He unpacked his small propane stove and set it on wire stilts.

He lit the blue flame of the stove and peeled back the cover of a sausage tin and poured the contents into a pan. The oily liquid spat and cussed.

"Watch your mouth," he said.

He took off his shell and fleece, lifted his shirt from his bare chest, and felt a sting as the cold air hit where the towrope had rubbed a red, weeping line into his stomach. Some skin had already begun peeling and in places his stomach looked like a bruised peach. He licked his fingers and rubbed saliva into the wound, then left his shirt cinched up above his belly so it could breathe.

He popped a hot sausage into his mouth, chewed, and looked at the tarp-wrapped body. The tarp had come loose on one side, revealing a light blue fist. He felt along the top of the hand and noticed, through the skin, the tracks of bones and tendons attached to the fingers.

"The funny thing is, I only ever wanted to be alone," he said and trailed off. He leaned over and tucked the yellow tarp into the places where it had escaped. "They hate me for it. They see me, and what they see is a threat. It's the nature of things, I suppose, to hate what you don't understand. And I suppose I've hated them, too."

He patted the body on the shoulder, lay down next to it, and closed his eyes.

"I don't hate them," he said. "They see something strange and their hackles raise. It's how they're supposed to be. It's a smart way to be, if you think about it."

He turned over and gave in to the sleep. Along with the rattling of brush and leaves, there was the sound of dogs barking on the wind, but he heard it in his dreams, if he heard it at all.

~

Walter shivered and woke. He sat up and spit and tried to take a drink from the water bottle, but he was only able to tongue a few drops because the rest had frozen. He took a silver canteen from the front pocket of his pack and sipped from it. He swished the rye whiskey around in his mouth, then swallowed. His eyes watered. He took off his gloves and checked his watch. He'd slept for two hours.

"It occurs to me, Anne, that this might only confirm what everyone thinks. That I'm no different than the dogs I keep."

He fingered one of the brass-ringed corners of the tarp and sighed.

"Which, now that I think about it, I agree with. I am an animal. The only difference is that they think they're something different. They see a deer or a tree or a hawk and call it nature, but they see themselves in the mirror and call it something else."

Outside, the wind huffed and snow dust skated across the frozen surface of the lake.

"I shouldn't speak like that," he said. "Like I'm different. Me talking like I'm on the outside looking in proves otherwise. Like I said, it's the nature of the world. I'm simply playing my part. They are, too. We give each other definition. We all do."

He gathered his things and pulled the sled from beneath the overhang. His breath quickened as he tried to situate the rope around his belly which still stung where a groove had been worn.

"Here's a question," he said. "What brought you all the way up here? Don't say the weather. Don't say luck, either.

Did they send you?"

The harsh, cutting sound of barking dogs erupted. He stopped and looked around. A few more barks split the morning quiet. He waited and listened. There was no sound for a while.

A Northern Flicker called out somewhere in the forest beyond. Half a dozen black Juncos flitted past the mouth of the overhang, tree-hopping and chit-chattering, happy in the still of the morning, moving further and further into the woods. He gathered everything and followed.

~

It was now eleven in the morning. Walter touched the rope on his belly and winced.

"There's no name for this, Anne. I know them. They won't know what to call this, so they'll call it something else they do know, whether it fits or not."

In the distance, the outline of an alpine cabin emerged from the fog. He trudged toward it and found no vehicles parked outside. No snow had been shoveled, either.

His stomach quivered as he removed the rope. After it dropped to the ground, he stood for a moment with his hands on his knees, watching his breath form clouds. Then he walked around the perimeter of the cabin, checking here and there, rubbing the frost off windows with his fist and peering inside. Everything was dark.

He went back, pulled the sled into the front yard, and pushed it beneath a large pine bordering the front porch.

"Stay here," he said. "I'll be back in a minute."

He unbuckled his snowshoe webs. He knocked a few times at the door. He peered again through the front window. He found a key hidden under an empty flower pot and let himself inside. In the kitchen, he retrieved a few bottles of water from the refrigerator and chugged one down. He searched the cabinets and found a box of macaroni and cheese and a jar of instant coffee. He made himself lunch.

He searched the cabin. It was built in the shape of the triangle roof which started at ground level and came to a point in what looked like a loft upstairs. The main floor hallway was lined with pictures. They were arranged along the hallway chronologically. He moved slowly down the hallway, through time in pictures, and watched the family grow up. He plucked one of the pictures from the wall, showing the family vacationing somewhere tropical, tan and beached and looking happy.

He replaced the picture, walked back outside, and pulled the sled holding the body from beneath the pine tree. He undid the wrapping and lifted the curled body up in his arms, then walked it back into the house and laid it down on the carpet next to the brown couch. He grabbed the canteen from his pack, poured another cup of coffee, and sat down on the couch next to the body. He took a long swig of whiskey, coughed, and chased it down with the coffee. He turned on the television. The Plinko game was on "The Price is Right." On the screen, a co-ed with a college sweatshirt joked with the host.

"These things; these circumstances. Once people think you're strange?" He took a small sip of whiskey and continued. "You don't know how hard it is to change how people think. If you try, they suspect you even more."

He took another sip of whiskey and a few gulps of coffee with it.

"The funny thing is," he said, "is that I was trying to do the right thing. No, I was doing the right thing. I stand by that, regardless of what anyone says. And the courts believed me, even if no one else did. The boy needed a place to stay was all. Some food. He was in a tight spot, the way he described it. A tight spot. And he was. That was more than evident."

The co-ed let go of a puck and it rushed down the board.

"But the kid wasn't ready to tell the truth about the real problem. It would've cost him too much. So he told a lie about me instead. And I understand that. I really do. I don't like it, but I understand it. Even in my situation now, I wouldn't change places with him, wherever he is. I imagine it's not a good place. I would have seen him by now if it was. He would have asked for my forgiveness. He would have cleared my name. I believe that, because he was a good boy. I could see it. I can see these things."

Another puck rushed down the board. The audience sighed.

"People see things the way they see them," Walter continued. "I most likely would have seen the same thing, were I them. It'd be arrogant of me to think otherwise. But I'm not them. Which they believe, but in a different way than I believe. Which is the problem, I suppose. I'm sorry. I've been over this. When you live like I do, you go over things until you're done with them, then you go over them again."

The co-ed let go of her last puck. It struggled down the Plinko board, stopping at every notch until it tilted at the bottom and dropped into the fifty-thousand-dollar slot. Confetti dropped, and she jumped and cheered as the host kept his composure.

Walter twisted shut the canteen as the television went to a commercial. "People been scared of me since I was a kid," he said. "It's in the eyes. The shoulders. The mouth." Walter shook his head. "It's in every dang thing."

He leaned back and didn't say anything for a while. His eyes began to flutter and close. Then they flipped back open again.

"I hope there's a God," he said. "Because He knows things. He knows how it is."

A dog barked somewhere out in the neighborhood. It was a sharp sound, jilted, cut off. It was followed by another bark, one that sounded more like a howl, one that moved in pitch from high to low and then disappeared into grovel.

"Except my dogs," he said. "They know, too. If I didn't have my dogs...I don't know."

He shifted in his seat, lost his breath, and touched his stomach. He tried to lift his shirt, but blood and pus had glued to the fabric and staunched the wound. He gritted his teeth and peeled it off. The thin gash had broadened. The edges of the wound were now red and inflamed and fluid had dripped down and soaked the rims of his pants. The wound had the look of a molten glacier, crust split apart.

He twisted open the canteen and poured a few drops of rye across the wound. He screamed.

~

Six hours later, Walter emerged from the forest. He stood on a hill overlooking a soccer field on the outskirts of town. He closed his eyes, bent over, massaged his calves and thighs, then stood back up. He gently touched the rope clinging to the ridge in his belly and gritted his teeth. He removed his cap because it had warmed considerably. The snowflakes landing on the sleeve of his parka quickly pearled into water.

"I'm tempted to leave you here," he said. "They'd find you soon enough." He looked over to the corner of the field where some kids were playing tackle football in the snow, bundled up stiff in caps and mittens and parkas and galoshes. Beyond them stood a thicket of houses split by streets. Afternoon was spent, and a hazy dusk had begun settling on the valley.

He took a long drink of rye from the canteen and a few longer gulps of water from the bottle. He pulled her wallet from his jacket, flipped it open, and checked the address. "I'm going to need to be a little drunk for this, Anne. You never know how it's going to be in town."

After one more slug of whiskey, Walter began crossing the field, body in tow.

The boys stopped playing football and watched. They crowded together, talked, and looked over at him some more.

Walter sped up and tried to keep from looking in their direction.

One of the kids broke off from the group and wandered over.

Walter changed his path and veered away, glancing again over his shoulder. The boy was jogging after him.

"Hey!" the boy yelled.

Walter didn't stop. "Don't come any closer," he said.

The boy didn't listen and kept coming. He looked more surprised than anything. "What are you doing?" the boy asked.

"Nothing."

Then the boy suddenly stopped. His face corrupted. He screamed and backed away and fell, then got back up and fled.

Walter looked down at the sled and saw that the edge of the tarp had somehow come loose, revealing that light blue hand curled into a fist.

The boy ran across the field and met the others by the goalpost. They huddled for a moment and then all began running.

Walter almost threw up. He bent over and waited for the churning in his stomach to stop. He folded the tarp back over the hand. He took a deep breath, muscled the last couple fingers of rye down his throat, and jogged across the field and across the street and down the parkway toward the center of town.

~

All of Walter's dogs gathered on the hill overlooking the now-empty soccer field. They sniffed the air and pawed the snow. The only visual evidence was the long, deep carve of the sled's tracks across the field, intersected by two scattered lines punched by the boy's feet.

One of the dogs let out a yip and then trotted down the hill into the field, following the impression made by the sled. The rest followed.

~

Her parents' house was a brown rambler with a station wagon outside. Walter lifted the rope from his belly, then leaned over and burped. He swayed, grabbed the railing, and pulled himself up to the front door.

He turned one last time to look at the body.

"I don't know how this ends," he said. "But you know how it happened. And my dogs know. I only wish you could have met my dogs."

He rang the doorbell.

The door opened. A wave of warm air scented with firewood and cigarettes rushed out. A young woman stood holding the doorknob. She was dressed in a green, knitted sweater loaded with buttons and pockets. Red irritations rimmed her eyes, and there were gray hollows beneath.

An unshaven man in a hooded sweatshirt appeared behind her. He looked as though he had either just woken up or never gone to sleep.

"Sorry to bother you," said Walter. He turned to the side and opened his shoulder. "I wanted to get to you soon as possible."

The woman tilted her head.

"Found her yesterday. Up by my house. Frozen solid. I dragged her down on my sled because we knew..."

The woman sunk down to her heels and put her hands out to steady herself on the porch.

The man rushed past her down the steps. He ripped at the tarp and the cords. He pulled the body from the sled and held it in his arms.

The woman crawled on her hands and knees across the landing and down the front steps. When she reached the body, she screamed.

Walter steadied himself against the doorframe. The heat from their house blew behind him and the dark wind howled outside. The nearly gray face of the girl rested on her father's shoulder.

Dogs barked in the distance.

Walter coughed and burped.

The man stood up. His arms were straight at his side and his fists were stones.

"What did you do?" he stammered.

Walter shifted his legs and held tight to the rail. "I told you," he said. "I found her on my property. My dogs found her—"

The man took two long steps up to the landing. He slugged Walter low in the belly, just above the belt. The impact made very little sound. Walter wheezed and bent over then crumpled to the ground.

The woman said nothing. She rocked back and forth with the body in her arms.

The man made like he was going to kick Walter, but he stopped himself. His shoulders sagged. He began to cry. He turned around and went back to his wife and daughter at the base of the steps. He knelt and held his hands out like he wanted to grab something.

~

Across the street, a married couple that had lived in the neighborhood for years watched from the bay windows of their master bedroom on the second floor of their house.

"I'm speechless," said the woman. "Did the police say how long it would take for them to get here?"

The man was about to answer when, from down the street, a pack of dogs appeared. There were dozens, all sizes, spread out but all streaming towards the house.

"Those are—my word," said the woman. "That must be—I didn't recognize him. That's Walter something or other. The guy who kidnapped the boy."

"He must have—"

The dogs rushed through the yard. The couple cowered and covered the body of their daughter with their hands and shoulders, but the dogs paid no attention to them. They milled past and circled Walter and bit his clothing and slowly began dragging him down the steps, then around the family and through the snow-covered front lawn. They pulled Walter down the sidewalk, back in the directions they came.

"I'm going to do something about this madness," said the man.

He left the room, and the woman stayed at the window, watching as the dogs continued pulling Walter's body down the sidewalk.

Then, below, her husband emerged from their house and tromped out into the snow, a shotgun in his hand. He whistled and yelled and followed the dogs.

"There isn't a name for it," said the woman.

Tusks

One day we all grew tusks, one pointing out from each cheek. Surprisingly few accommodations needed to be made. Motorcycle helmets, scuba gear—any solid thing wrapped around the face no longer worked. But other than that, we got used to them. Sleep was not a problem because no one really ever sleeps face down. Blowing one's nose was difficult, and kissing was shot, but eating was okay.

Soon we began to enjoy the tusks. We shined and buffed them. We illustrated and tagged them. We etched the names of our loved ones through the enamel. We carved religious texts and memorials and celebrity profiles into the dentine. We invented outfits for them, for when we went to the office, parties, and so on. Soon, we imagined our ancestors having them. Then we imagined aliens having them. Finally, we imagined God having them. It was then that we all made a pact and cut them off. It was then that we grew tails.

Ripe

One otherwise forgettable night a few years ago, Raleigh Stowell's ears transformed into ripe, misshapen, pockmarked mandarin oranges and never changed back. There were a few others like him in the world, but too few to stop his situation from being universally thought of as strange and, for some, scary. But unlike most everyone else, his coworker, Meg Treadwell, didn't seem to mind his ears; in fact, rumors about Raleigh's and Meg's affection for one another had been circling the office in Dubuque for months. It took Raleigh that long to muster the courage to ask her out, and even then, he still waited.

Aside from the normal attractions—kindness, intelligence, beauty—what made her compelling to Raleigh was also what made her a strange mystery: she was never without gloves. Even in the office restroom, instead of washing in one of the sinks, she would stay in the stall and rub sanitizing lotion into her hands in private. No one had actually seen her do this, of course, but a coworker deduced it from the disinfectant scent the lotion would leave. Raleigh wanted to understand why she did this and also what lay behind the sadness sometimes in her eyes: an exhaustion; a fatigue. He'd come over to her desk only to find her trying to wipe her face of tears. Nothing was wrong, she'd tell him. Her eyes were irritated from her makeup. Payment for her vanity.

But alongside his curiosity and desire to understand and share in her pain, there was an even more simple reason for his attraction: her voice was a crystalline bell, and when the sound hit his orange ears, no matter how low his mood, he felt unreasonable delight.

The two of them were slated to give a presentation together on the nuances of bookkeeping at the annual agricultural trade show held in Seattle. His heart ached in such a way that he finally decided he could wait no longer, so he resolved to confess his feelings to her there. On the flight from Dubuque, sitting next to each other with legs stretched out in an exit row, their conversation never paused, sliding between diverse topics with ease, ranging from top-ten sitcoms to childhood regrets to her painful divorce five years earlier. Meanwhile, above, in the overhead bin, stapled together in the binder of his briefcase, was a ten-page, singled-spaced letter confessing his love, a treatise he'd worked on for over a month, crafted to perfection with the help of a freelance editor whose information he'd found tacked to a corkboard at the local library.

That first night, after the opening meet-and-greet with the other participants, he slid the letter beneath Meg's hotel room door before hurrying away.

Since then, he hasn't slept.

~

Now, it's morning. They sit next to each other at a round table in the crowded cafeteria of the trade show, reflecting on the amenities in their hotel rooms. Both are dressed for their presentation—her in a dark-gray pantsuit with a lime-green blouse, him with a gray wool sweater and tan slacks. At the center of the table rests a basket filled with melons and thick-crusted breads laid atop green and red holiday ribbons. Across from them, an older couple, likely farmers, slice a small cantaloupe in half with a bread knife and begin scooping out the pulp with spoons.

At a break in the conversation, Raleigh takes a sip of black coffee from his travel thermos and clears his throat. "Did you get my letter?"

Speaking over the conversational hum, she says with her lovely voice that yes, she did, and it was a beautiful letter, and it made her cry, and she is flattered, it is a gift, no one has ever said these sorts of things to her before. But then she pauses, puts her gloved hands on the table, and gently presses her fingertips together. "Raleigh, I feel terrible. The truth is, I've always thought of us more as friends."

"Ah," Raleigh says, leaning back.

She takes a deep breath, brushes her hair from her temples with her palms—revealing her normal ears—and says, "But like I said, thank you for the wonderful letter. And for being so cool about this." She gestures back and forth between them. "You know."

"Of course. No problem. I won't be weird about it." He reaches into his briefcase for a folder. "Well, let's go over this presentation one more time."

~

After the presentation—a success—and an awkward goodbye, Raleigh doesn't go to another breakout session because he fears seeing Meg again, having to hear her graceful voice, and feeling the pain it would cause. It took courage to believe that, maybe this one time, his orange ears wouldn't prevent him from experiencing companionship. He wishes, as he has many times before, that he could surgically remove them without losing his hearing. Now he wonders if, in the end, the trade would be worth it. Perhaps a silent world would be better than a loveless one. *But then I wouldn't hear her lovely voice*, he thinks. *But then she might show me her hands.*

He doesn't want to be alone in his hotel room, so he wanders up the carpeted staircase to the conference bar, satchel slung over his shoulder. He slumps down on a stool and orders a jack-and-coke. A contemplative holiday mix plays in the background. Everyone around is smiling and wearing dress clothes creased here and there from travel. Overtures are being made; he can hear one in progress three barstools down. Another couple turns and stares at him before looking away. *Yes,* he thinks. *Exactly. Everyone stares at me and everyone eventually looks away.*

He begins to laugh, first at how melodramatic that sounds, then for the absurdity of thinking he could date Meg. It will be yet another Christmas without company, save a few Zoom calls with family members in other states. After he laughs for a while, the bartender—a young woman with a slew of colorful bangles on both wrists—comes to ask if he's okay.

"I'm great. Swell. This is the life!"

She glances at his ears, ducks down to get the liquor, and makes him another jack-and-coke, this time on the house. "I hope it improves."

Before he can start in on the second drink, he feels a tap on the shoulder. He turns and finds the couple that had been staring at him. It's Deborah Burgeon—she has a nametag—and her husband, Wayne, both dressed like golfers at a municipal course, wearing short-sleeved collared shirts and cargo pants. They begin to question him about his ears. Are the oranges a joke? Special earmuffs? They're real? How do they feel? Has your hearing been impaired in any way? And so on. The questioning normally would have bothered him, but right now he doesn't really care about anything.

"My. What a world this is," says Deborah, reaching up to adjust a rhinestone necklace askew on her collar. "Well, I have to ask. How is it being this way, really?"

Wayne takes off his denim Kern County Ag hat and curves the brim in his palms. "Honey–"

"It's a valid question," she says. "I'm trying to draw him out. All he's given us so far are facts."

"Deb…"

"Honestly," Raleigh says, "it can suck. For instance, I just got rejected because of them, so I'm doing the drinking thing tonight. Again."

"Yeah, I imagine those ears are a dealbreaker." She takes out her purse and slaps a twenty on the counter. "Let us buy you the next couple. You've earned a bender. But in the meantime, come on. Don't B.S. your aunt Deb. Spill your heart on the counter. I'll catch it."

Wayne puts his hand on Deborah's shoulder. "Darling, let's let the man…"

"Let me put it this way," she continues. "It seems to me that you have a choice between looking like you do and having no chance at love, or being deaf but with prospects."

Raleigh downs the rest of the drink and shakes the glass, making the ice rattle. "That about sums it up."

"Well, your move is clear. You've got to get rid of

them. Love is more important than hearing. You can just use closed captioning when you watch the tv, and it's better that way, anyway. We always have the closed captioning on, even when the sound's on."

"That's insensitive, Deb," says Wayne.

"Look Raleigh," she says, "what I'm saying is, our marriage has lasted thirty-five years, and Wayne here, well, you see him. You've experienced him."

Wayne shakes his head.

"Whatever you decide, let me know. We live in the San Joaquin Valley, and my cousin's friend is a key grip in Hollywood. He could pass your situation by a producer, and maybe they'd do a documentary. Hold off on deciding about the ears until I get back to you. They might want to film a before and after."

Deb and Wayne leave holding hands. He takes out his phone and, wanting to feel worse—if only to get it over with—he begins scanning the pictures on Meg's Instagram wall and watching her Reels. After a few intense minutes, he can't stand seeing and hearing her anymore, so he looks up surgeons, as well as accounts of their surgeries, of which there are only a few.

He sets down his phone and closes his eyes, listening to all the noise. The clinks of glasses and silverware. The laughter. The holiday music playing in the background. He imagines quiet—perpetual silence—and it makes him afraid. He wonders if it will make him feel just as alone as the ears, only in a different way. Sound is a kind of company, and he'd lose even that.

~

Three hours later, sugary drunk and emotional, Raleigh trudges down the steps from the bar toward the lobby and takes the elevator up to the wrong floor. He eventually finds the right one and makes it down the matte cream hallway to his room, touching walls as a crutch. As he's struggling to get the plastic key card into the slot, he hears footfalls behind him. He turns and sees Meg.

She's changed from her work clothes into a University of Iowa sweater and jeans. She holds her hands behind her back, and something about that makes her look distraught. "Hi."

Her voice. Just one word from her, and he reconsiders the surgery. "Are you okay?" he asks, listing to the side a bit.

Her eyes move to his eyes, his ears, his chest. "Are you?"

"I'm just really drunk. I should say that up front, before whatever conversation happens here."

She smiles. "I'm a little drunk, too."

"It's what happens," he says.

She nods, solemn. "Raleigh, I have something to tell you. The truth is, I lied to you earlier." She looks down before looking back up, worried.

"Wait. What do you mean?"

"I just got it in my head that it couldn't work."

He tries for a moment to put it together. "I don't understand. You mean..."

"I mean I'm in love with you." She's on the verge of tears. "But I have something I need to show you. Something that might change your mind about me." She holds out her hands—they're shaking—and begins picking at the tips of her gloved fingers until the gloves loosen and slide off. He can't believe what he sees. Her shaking fingers are strings of violet grapes. Light reflects off their skins like tiny open windows.

"I know," she says. "It's hideous."

"I wouldn't change a word of my letter."

They stand there, blushing. Nat King Cole croons softly from the hallway speakers. Someone walks by; neither of them notices. If a dozen people walked by, they'd still think they were alone.

She looks at him and says, "I'd get them removed, but I'd lose all feeling."

He puts his hand up to his ears. "I'd lose all hearing." He reaches and takes her hand. Her grape fingers are smooth and moist from the tears, and he slides his thumbs along their hills and valleys.

"It's been so, so long since I've touched anyone," she says. "My ex-husband, he wouldn't..." She pulls her hand away and wipes her eyes and nose with the sleeve of her sweatshirt. Then she looks back and forth between his orange ears. "Can I touch them?"

He nods. She reaches up. It tickles, and he can't help but laugh. She laughs, too. They don't really know what to do next. There is so much to hear. There is so much to feel.

The Failure

He was the kind of person who, while chopping onions at a friend's party, proceeds to cut off his own finger—knuckles and all—and immediately, with thought to nothing else, worries how the host might react to the mess. The mess: a threat to his standing, an affront to his self-respect, the blood proof of his inability to do a simple task without injuring himself to the point of needing medical attention. The party would soon break up, and he'd be the cause. The stump could heal, but a wound to one's status was stubborn, and his status was already suspect, what with the elimination of the career he hated—the one he needed for occasions such as this, where financial success was proof of one's worth. He was now broke, and thus, irrelevant. But right then, as he stood there on the shale tile in this beautiful, rational kitchen, sink now pink with his blood, he gloved his hand with a towel, sat down, and called the medics, leaving the growing mess to someone else, someone not bleeding—maybe the host, who was currently discussing a recent trip to coastal Spain, who was the kind of person who committed his life to having a massive, elegant headstone, etched with noble words, words that wouldn't be read by anyone past the grandchildren, yes, yet another person who did good things to the right people and saved up for a killer grave. The kind of person he'd himself been until this very moment, when he'd lost something valuable in order to find something important: a dead finger, unattached, in the sink, pointing at him.

s Crash Into the Water That Becomes Them

I am named after my father, Noel Blaintive, a good man who hid from me his entire life. For the longest time, I could never understand why he hid. I would say as much at his funeral two years ago, after he died alone of a stroke while having cobb salad in a hotel room at a conference center in San Francisco. He designed passenger seats for airplanes but never talked about it at home.

We found a receipt in his pocket from the day before he died. He'd boarded one of those tour boats for a morning cruise out in San Francisco Bay. He loved the water. At a younger age, he was a surfer, a hobby I took on myself—my children have as well. He used to tell me facts about water: that the same amount of it is on Earth as when the dinosaurs roamed; that Earth's water came from comets and asteroids; that there is more water in the atmosphere than in all of Earth's rivers combined. These truths made him happy in a way the rest of his life didn't.

~

One night, when I was in seventh grade, I planned to use my father's flathead screwdriver to pry the hood ornament from my neighbor Leonard Rosenblum's old BMW, stealing with it the respect of a few other boys my age. The clear plastic handle of the screwdriver stuck up from the back pocket of my jeans. Through the blinds, splitting the bedroom window of my home, the sun had nearly set, pinks and purples and blues fading into one another, borders fluid. I stood watching. I'd been invited to meet with the boys the next morning at the playground to compare what we'd stolen, and I had nothing yet, but there by the window, I had hope. I thought of the boys and what they would think if I was finally the one, as they say, with a story to tell.

Once it was dark enough, I laced up my shoes and went downstairs into the living room. What I remember about our house is how the popcorn ceilings always felt too low, the light too dim. A fake Persian rug lay on thin, cream-colored carpeting, couches tan, and I could hear my sister practicing her scales down the hallway on her rental saxophone. My mother, Kathy, was president of the PTA and attending its weekly meeting, but my father sat in his brown corduroy chair, leaning forward, face in his hands, hair short and tidy, still wearing slacks and a collared shirt, unaware of my presence. He talked quietly but urgently to himself, rubbing his hairy arms. I caught the words 'fuck' and 'Jesus Christ,' intermingled with others, nearly coughs, unintelligible. You could feel the grinding of his teeth in the words. He wasn't drowning, but he was below the water.

~

Once, at a younger, more innocent age, in the middle of one of my father's fits of swearing, I asked him who he was swearing at. He looked up and examined me, as if he was surprised by so direct a question, perhaps surprised that anyone had noticed. I wondered if he even realized he was doing it. "I'm swearing at myself," he said. "You shouldn't swear at other people. Our family doesn't do that."

~

There in the living room, after my father noticed my presence and stopped swearing, he put his hands on his knees, sat back, and forced a smile. "Hey buddy."

"I'm going out for a walk."

"A walk? It's a little late. Finished your homework?"

"Yeah."

"Good." He nodded his head. "Good. Want company?"

That he'd asked me was more kind than I realized. I could tell he didn't feel like going on a walk with me. It might have been the last thing he wanted to do, but he wanted to be the sort of father who went on walks with his son. Another way of putting it is he wanted me to have that kind of father. My father's love was different than the kind most talk about these days, that of love being a strong, emotional desire to fulfill. His love was the kind that compelled a person to do what they only wished they wanted to do.

I held up my portable cassette tape player—a birthday present—and said, "Think I'm going to listen to music."

He nodded again, crossed his legs, and picked up the still-coiled *Seattle Times* from the side table, the evening edition. He slid off the rubber bands.

~

When my father died, my mother was beside herself with grief, so I was the one who looked through his emails, trying to make sure to find as many people he knew as possible so we could let them know what had happened to him. We found jovial correspondences with friends we'd never heard of before. I sent messages to everyone, telling them the date and time of the funeral.

A few came to the funeral and told us stories. One friend knew him from his days in Berkeley—he'd only ever mentioned living in San Francisco after college—and I found out my father had been a hippy. After the funeral potluck which we held in a white-walled classroom in the rec center near my parent's house, a woman in a bright purple shawl and pumpkin orange shirt touched my arm. I was ladling myself some vodka lemonade punch. Once I finished, she told me she knew my father before he got married and moved to Seattle. Her name was Lark. She spilled a handful of pictures from her purse.

What I saw stunned me. It was like I'd been shown proof that I didn't really know him. Beyond the loose shirts, long hair, and tight jeans, he was grinning, earnest and intent. One photo showed him in the living room of some disheveled apartment, shirtless, seated on the edge of the couch, spliff in his mouth, intently watching Bob Dylan play a beat-up Gibson dreadnought. I couldn't believe it. Another was of him in an open field, long hair fanned over his shoulders, smiling like a fool. She told me they used to take trips to Table Mountain Ranch. "He hated LSD," she said. "He was one of those natural guys. He'd only take Peyote and grass." Then she handed me a picture of him at the beach wearing only blue swim trunks, standing with a longboard twice his size next to him, its nose sticking up into the air.

"He loved that most of all," she said.

"He did."

"Did he keep shaping?"

It took me a second to realize she meant shaping surfboards. "No, did he used to?"

She squinted at me and began to shake her head. "Your father hid some of what he loved."

I said nothing.

"But I bet he knew everything about you." She winked at me and nodded. "That was his way." She handed me the pictures. "I wish I had more to give you. Your father was one of the gentlest men I've ever known. I'm guessing he never told you that, for a while, he had hopes of becoming a monk. Shaping surfboards and meditation, that's what he wanted his life to be about. But he could never live that lifestyle for long. Everyone knew it."

"Were you guys..."

"We were lovers. But I was wild, idealistic, full of passion. I wanted him to move to a commune with me, maybe even start one ourselves. He told me he did, too, but I think the reality scared him too much. I think he thought it would be selfish of him. And who knows? Maybe for him, he was right."

~

Night air cooling, I walked a handful of blocks toward Leonard Rosenblum's house and his old BMW with my hands in the front pockets of my jeans. The hills of our neighborhood didn't so much roll as pitch. This was a bedroom community in the north of Seattle, and it had no storefronts, only the occasional church or synagogue. Houses upon houses built with brick in the 50s on land taken from Native Americans lay wedged together like so many boxes of nails lined up and stacked in hardware stores like the one my father had sometimes taken me to. I turned down a quiet street and saw Leonard, a novelist who wore jeans, hiking boots, and a ribbed sweater. Leonard had two kids under the age of ten. Often, I'd see them bouncing on a huge trampoline in the front yard while he read on the steps. I took off my headphones, feeling like I'd already been caught. I couldn't quite see his face in the dark.

"Noel Junior. Why are you out here so late? Not that I'm one to talk."

"Just listening to music." My father spoke of Leonard with respect—he had a few of his novels in the bookcase in the living room. I'd once opened one and read the first pages. They bored me, but to write a book still seemed like magic to me, like Coltrane playing saxophone through the stereo in my sister's room. I feared that Leonard, with this magic, knew what I was planning to do.

"Okay," he said. "Well, enjoy, and give my regards to your folks."

Leonard left, and I took a deep breath and put my headphones back on, then wiped sweat from my upper lip and brow. I was nervous. I crossed the winding street and up the graded top of the hill. There weren't many European cars in our neighborhood, at least not yet—it would be another five years or so before the first technological boom, making this neighborhood desirable for its proximity to Microsoft and the companies following it. I slowed my pace as I approached Leonard's house. On the North side was a carport, alongside which stood a row of evergreen hedges marking the property line. I figured I could hide in there if I heard anyone coming.

I saw faint light through the window adjacent to the

carport, but the drapes mostly concealed it. I checked up and down the street but saw nothing. I crept along the hedgerow, shoulders brushing the many-fingered leaves—their scent a biting green—until I came to the white BMW. I stood there for a few moments, feeling awful for what I was about to do. I could feel guilty for something I hadn't yet done. This was a fault I shared with my father, small but important—minor faults can still shape a life. I pushed my feelings aside as best I could. It would be worse to show up to the park with nothing and then leave there alone again.

I wiped my hand over the smooth surface of the hood ornament—no dust, it had been recently washed—and studied it: a black ring with BMW in white letters wrapped around a simple pattern of white and blue pie quarters, like pieces from the Trivial Pursuit game I'd occasionally played with my family at Thanksgiving. I had just begun trying to wedge the head of the screwdriver into the base of the emblem when I heard my name. My body prickled like static. I recognized the voice. It was Leonard.

"Find a Buick instead," he said. "Those ones on the Beamers are tough to get off." He came into the dim light of the carport, smiling. "Go on, get out of here. I'm not going to call the police. But I am going to call your father when I go inside, so he'll be expecting you."

I walked slowly home, my pulse beating hard in my ears. I passed the house next door to our own and saw my father standing beneath our porch light, hand over his eyebrows, looking out. Up to that point, it hadn't occurred to me that by stealing a hood ornament I was betraying his trust and our family's name, but I felt it. Young people feel the truths that only later they'll understand.

I climbed the cement steps to our house and my father looked at me, or rather, he examined me—like he had those years ago when I'd asked him why he swore at himself. But he didn't swear. In his eyes and brows there was curiosity, like he was trying to figure me out. He opened the door and, confused, I walked past him into the house. The door clicked shut behind me, and I waited while my father closed the drapes in silence. With his back facing me, he told me to sit down on the sofa. I did.

He sat down in his corduroy chair opposite me, leaned forward, and took a deep breath. "I'm not angry, but I am confused. I just never thought that you, of all people, would try to steal a hood ornament, and from Leonard's car."

He'd misjudged me. He'd thought I was someone else. Who was I now to my father? "I'm sorry. I'm really sorry. I just—"

"As I was waiting for you to come home, I thought to myself, 'There has to be a reason for this. The Noel I know would never do this sort of thing without a reason.' And I thought to myself, 'This probably has to do with his new friends.'"

I said nothing.

"Do you have the screwdriver?" he asked.

I pulled it from my back pocket and tried to hand it over.

He didn't take it. Instead, he stood from his chair and began walking toward the hallway. He stopped at the top of the steps down to the garage. He flipped on the light. "C'mon."

I followed him down, seeing the receding hair on the crown of his head from above. I tried to figure out what he was doing. He wasn't angry, and he'd never so much as spanked me, so I didn't fear him in that way. I felt more disoriented. He opened the door to the garage and turned on the lights, the room now bathed in shallow yellow. Inside were lines of shelves filled with boxes and old equipment and toys, as well as a small worktable where my father had helped me build a pine box derby car. The room smelled of sweet, fresh cut wood. From the rack above the table, he retrieved a flashlight, and from a wooden box, he grabbed a small hammer.

Filling up most of the garage was my father's aging brown Oldsmobile. It didn't have the makeshift roof rack he later built because he hadn't picked up surfing again, not yet, because my sister and I weren't old enough to be taught. He walked to the hood of the car and handed the flashlight to me. "Hold this steady. Point it at the hood." The ornament shone in the light, sticking up from the car, a rectangular blue and red coat of arms circled by a silver ring. He held out his hand, palm up. "Screwdriver."

I hesitated, struggling to believe what was happening.

"Give it to me."

"Why are you doing this?"

"Give me the screwdriver."

I handed it over.

With his left hand, he pressed the blade of the screwdriver into the base of the hood ornament. He took a short, sharp swing with the hammer—it clacked against the plastic handle, like a cue ball striking the eight—and the screwdriver dug beneath the hard plastic base. The sound of it all was terrible.

"Dad..."

"Quiet." He hammered again, and again, and again,

until the screws of the base tore up and out. He yanked off the hood ornament, switched hands, and looked at his palm. He was bleeding. He wiped it off on his jeans and handed the hood ornament to me.

~

Years later, I met Leonard Rosenblum at a reading in the downtown library in Seattle where I still lived. Afterward, we sat in a booth across from each other while couples dressed for the symphony across the street walked past us down the aisle. It was busy, but still quiet. He now lived in New York, but he was on a tour promoting the paperback edition of his novel that had been a finalist for the National Book Award. By that time, I was an author myself, and to my surprise, he told me he'd read my book and had been meaning to reach out to me. We went out for drinks after the reading and discussed agents and editors and publishing and, eventually, the conversation turned to a scene in his book.

"So I've been meaning to ask you. Did I get it right?" he said. "The hood ornament scene, I mean."

I told him what he didn't know about that night—my father, the Oldsmobile—and I told him he wasn't allowed to use that part of the story, because it was in a novel I'd started.

"I won't even mention it to Janet, though she would be touched. But you must thank me for my silence in the acknowledgments."

"You didn't thank me in yours."

He laughed. "I will pay it back, Noel. You now have me in your corner."

I nodded, and a waiter came to our table. We each ordered another drink—me a pint of pale ale, him a scotch on the rocks. He checked his phone, tapped the screen a few times, and turned his attention back to me. "Your father. I talked to him dozens of times, but now that I look back, I realize I never really knew him. And from what you've told me, I would have wanted to know him."

"No one around here knew my father."

"Do you think he knew himself?"

I paused. "I don't know. Maybe too well."

~

Yesterday I visited my mother in the same home I grew up in. I haven't spoken of her at length until now for this reason: my father never told her about the hood ornament. He'd blamed it on some neighbor kid. I was there in the kitchen when he did it. His explanation gave me relief and shame.

My mother and I sat beneath a patio umbrella in the garden in the backyard, drinking chai tea and talking, mostly about my kids, whom she loved with a passion. The air smelled of lavender from the bushes surrounding us— their tall, purple-flowered stalks drooping beneath the weight of the bees gathering their pollen, only to sway back up when the bees took flight. My father had been dead for two years. I told her about Lark, my father's old lover, and asked if she remembered her, and told her about him wanting to be a monk and shape surfboards.

"Lark was a prima donna," my mother said, reaching out to take her teacup before changing her mind. She wore a blue-and-white checkered sundress and wraparound sunglasses she'd probably bought at a drugstore. "Your father loved her, but in a different way than he did me. When you love someone, you also love who you are with that person. He couldn't love who he was with her, though I think he wanted to." She stopped and coughed into her fist, then wiped off her hand with her napkin. "That's why he couldn't open a surfboard shop. That's why he couldn't be a monk. He loved me deeply. Of that I have no doubt. But unlike Lark, he also wanted to be who he was with me. With us."

There's who a person wants to be, and who they are, and in some lives those two through lines can't ever intersect because so much of their meaning comes from not being the other. "Did that bother you?"

She pursed her lips and squinted at me for a moment, thinking. "It did in the beginning. Yes. I was a little threatened by it at times, that there was a part of him that could love a person like Lark, but it was also what attracted me to him. He wasn't like me." Then she told me what I already knew: that she'd always been an open book, that she'd never had much conflict in her heart. That she wanted to marry my father, so she did. That she wanted to have kids, so she did. That she wanted to be a homemaker, a PTA president, a good neighbor, so she was. "Your father, though. He was split in two. The sad thing is he was the one doing the splitting."

A helicopter slowly flew by overhead, and it was too loud to talk, so each of us took a sip of our tea and waited for it to pass.

"I told him," she continued, "that I would have followed him if he wanted to quit his job and do something more risky. But he didn't want that. That's why he quit shaping."

"But he'd let himself surf."

"Because he could justify it by teaching you and your sister. He never would have picked up a board without you."

~

I wish I could say that I didn't carry that hood ornament to the park the morning after I stole it and flash it to everyone like a book I'd written and was waiting to sign. I wish I could tell you it didn't gain me the respect I so wanted. My new friends treated me differently. Better. Still, I couldn't be like them, not for long, no matter how hard my father tried to help me—in fact, his attempt to help made certain of that. He might as well have ripped off one of my fingers when he ripped off that hood ornament. He'd taught me both what it was like to steal and what it was like to be stolen from.

After he died, when they found the ticket for the morning cruise in his pocket, they also found my father's leather bifold wallet, thick with credit cards and business cards and receipts whose ink had faded. But there was a worn picture inside as well, of my mother and me sitting on the hood of that old Oldsmobile with the void where the hood ornament used to be between us. We're both smiling and squinting, the evening sun casting a shadow across half our faces. I think of my father taking the picture, his face half in shadow, too.

When I turned sixteen, I learned to drive in that car, and it became mine when I got a job at the local supermarket. I used half of my paycheck each month to pay my parents back. Most of the time, when I drove, that hole in the hood and how it came about never entered my mind, but every so often, I would see it, and picture my father in the dim light, a hammer in one hand and a screwdriver in the other, teaching me what it meant to be a father who sacrificed his own dignity for his son's foolish game. For this reason, it took me a long time before I'd allow myself to be a novelist—to think it wasn't just another foolish game only made possible by the sacrifice of others, of people like my father. The novel I was writing— the one I told Leonard Rosenblum about, where my father steals his own hood ornament—never sold, but it no longer mattered. By that point I had to write, regardless of the outcome. My father never got to that point, perhaps because his own father had taught him what he taught me. I'll never know.

~

Driving home from having tea with my mother, I remembered the first time—but not the last—that I came out to Westport with my father to surf. The trip was a couple of years after he stole the hood ornament off his own car and gave it to me. We were catching the waves that broke off the brown rocks of the northern jetty, and it was foggy, like it often was there on the coast in early June. We were dressed in slick black wetsuits and floated in the lineup beyond the breakers. No one else was around, and between sets, it was quiet. We rose and fell with the swells.

He coughed, splashed some water onto his face, and said, "Noel, it just occurred to me: waves crash into the water that becomes them. You think about that." A koan a monk might say. He smiled curiously, as if he believed it, but not enough to make it his life. Then he turned and paddled away.

I never heard him swear in the ocean.

American Ice

Chips flew as I kicked a foothold with my left crampon. Same when I buried my right axe into the ice above my head. Crampon. Axe. Crampon. Axe. As I moved slowly up the chandelier, cool air wafting from the ice chilled my face. Below, the barren stony riverbed seemed to shrink as I ascended.

Above, Justin's wiry frame spread out across a small crevasse lit turquoise by the sun. I heard him cough and clear his nose. We'd made the decision to go ice climbing the night before, after performing in nearby Pratt. This was 2012, maybe '13. The show was packed, but deceptively full, as we sometimes said, because filling space in a small bar like that can feel celebratory until you split the take between four people. We stayed drunk and cocky all night, trying to strain every last bit of life out of the situation because a dive bar in Pratt wasn't a place we'd ever imagined performing. To me, it represented the logical end of a long series of stupid decisions.

And here we were, manifesting another by attempting to climb Mother of Pearl, a route in the North Cascades, in early May. I could feel it in the sun heating my bare neck. I could hear it in the ice dripping all around me.

~

Earlier, on the shoulder of the highway overpass—Mother of Pearl in the background and the occasional car, truck, and semi hurtling below—Justin and I had argued out whether to climb. He said we should go ahead; what the hell, winter hadn't finished saying goodbye. Only a couple of days had broken fifty, even in the lowlands. I suggested that, instead, we hit up that climbing wall back in Ballard because—oh yeah—all the ice climbing routes had been officially closed for weeks.

"What do they know?" Justin said. "You only live once, man. Don't be a chicken shit. Think how cool it would be if we did."

These lines of argument were of the same substance as the ones I'd repeatedly given in to over the last decade: a series of concessions that had lengthened our music careers from three solid years to three solid years with a decade-long, slowly spiraling retirement tour. Musicians in our genre had a shelf life, and there was clear evidence that our use-by dates had passed.

But Justin didn't believe in anything that pragmatic, and honestly, I hadn't wanted to, either. The show in Pratt, however, confirmed the doubts that had been simmering inside of me: our time was up.

So, on the overpass, I agreed to climb Mother of Pearl, that way I would have the opportunity to tell Justin goodbye in a setting where he wouldn't be able to escape.

~

Dangling from the ice a half-mile from the road, I could still hear the hum of traffic, and it comforted me for a moment, even though it shouldn't have. No one could see us or hear us, nor would anyone assume that someone would be climbing this late in the year.

I felt a little breeze on my shoulder. With it came the pleasant, nipping smell of sap. I looked over my shoulder and found that we had nearly reached eye level with the fingertips of the cedars and firs lining Mother of Pearl's slowly rising stream.

"Cory, hurry the hell up," Justin called from above. He kicked the toe of a crampon into the ice, sending a glinting shower of bits down on me.

I couldn't wait to tell him I was done. I swung my axe and continued up.

~

Someone had named this route Mother of Pearl because glacier runoff colored the frozen flow a milky gray, but when the sun hit the ice just right, it reflected more complexity than clear ice formations. Ever seen the inside of an abalone shell? Like that.

I loved the sharp air, the battered hands, the tangy smell of the ice axe, how wool stinks when it gets sweaty. I loved how, every winter, the routes changed slightly because the ice would melt differently. I loved thinking about how the water had stopped mid-flow, as though it was resting part way towards its destination, and how the river's sleep provided us an opportunity to scamper up its sides. The ice would remain motionless all winter, and I imagined the water wondering if it would ever again move, ignorant of the truth that, once spring came, it would melt and continue on its way toward the ocean to meet up with the water that'd left it behind five months earlier.

Justin loved getting to the top. He couldn't care less about the stink of wool or the tang of steel or any precious metaphors. So long as there was ice to climb and the top remained out of reach, he stayed motivated and

considered every disappointment an opportunity that—
spun right—could help him get there.

For a long time, I admired him for being so fucking
optimistic about the band. I wished I could feel the same
way, and sometimes managed to come close with his help.
But now, his optimism appeared to me as foolish, the
energy he insisted we spend felt like a waste, and every
opportunity seemed much more beneficial to the provider.

~

Halfway up the chandelier, after the fourth pitch, we
rested on a flat hump and surveyed the forestland spread
out below. The wind cooled the sweat on my back. It felt
good. The sunlight had burned off most of the lighter
clouds, but some thick cumulonimbus zeppelins still
charged through the sky, changing the air temperature
fifteen degrees when they blocked the sun. One had just
moved in. I took off my sunglasses.

"What did you think of the show last night?" I asked,
while emptying my canteen and stuffing more ice inside to
melt, adding a drop of iodine to be safe.

"It was fun," he said.

"Not exactly The Showbox."

"We'll be back there soon enough," he said, his wry
smile telling me to be patient. I'd seen that same smile too
many times to count. We'd danced around this
conversation too many times to count.

"That's the thing," I said, about to commence the
retirement speech I'd rehearsed a hundred times before.
Just then, a series of pops erupted beneath us, sounding
like gunshots. From above, we heard a low, ghostly moan.

The chandelier. Mother.

"Maybe we should stop," I said.

"We're fine." He laughed, hopping to his feet and pulling his pack over his shoulders. His 'biners clinked against each other on his thigh. "She's still sleeping. Just snoring a bit."

"I don't know, man. I kind of think we should head down," I said.

"Down? Spine, Cory, spine! Anyways, it'll take just as long to finish climbing up."

I took a sip of water. From behind a billowy cloud, the sun reemerged, hot on my chest. I put my sunglasses back on.

Justin sighed and checked his watch, which pissed me off. I wanted to set him straight, right then and there. But the timing was wrong. We needed to move, now. I'd give him the speech on top, provided we made it. He'd be in a great mood. We'd have the whole hike down to discuss how to dissolve the band.

It was my turn to lead a pitch. We decided it would be best to shimmy ten yards to the left before ascending because the ice above us was taking direct sunlight and looked sketchy. I drilled a screw into a firm section, threaded the rope through, and tossed it over to Justin so he could belay me. He hammered in a stopper and grabbed the rope with his gloved hands.

I wiped a small line of sweat from my sunglasses and drove an axe into the sheer ice above my head. I inched over. The ice to my left had seen no sunlight and still bulged thick and bulbous. I wanted to follow that strand up to the top.

A few staccato pops sang out near where Justin sat.

"She's burping," he yelled.

Everything was funny with Justin. When some manager screwed us out of most of our take, he chuckled. When our second album received four-out-of-ten on Pitchfork and they stopped reviewing anything else we released, the joke was on them. When I reminded him that we'd gone from headlining fifteen-hundred-person venues in Los Angeles to entertaining forty-five people at dive bars, he'd start into *Ring of Fire*, then name off every other artist who'd staged an epic comeback.

I swung my left axe, felt it lodge, and continued in the same manner, spidering sideways until I hugged a pillar in the middle of the route we'd chosen.

"Stay right there for a second," said Justin. With one hand, he rustled in his pack for the camera while the other held the rope. "You look like you're straddling an ice rocket. This will be great online."

"Hurry," I said.

I looked over my shoulder. The river weaved through the valley, faintly green where shallow, the color of asparagus where deep. Beyond, cars and trucks sped along the highway, their hum now barely audible as it mixed with the sound of running water. Below, the ice fanned lumpy and confused like a massive tree stump with part of its root base spread ominously above ground.

Then the ice beneath me groaned. My equipment rattled and, with a jolt, the section of ice I clung to slipped a couple of feet, then stopped. It felt like getting rear-ended. My stomach pressed up into my throat. I gripped both my axes as tight as I could, but what they held onto had begun teetering. I felt disoriented, weightless. I wanted to grab something, but there was nothing solid within reach. To move risked disturbing what little balance remained. My bones thrummed as the ice beneath me bellowed.

"Don't move, man. Don't move!" yelled Justin.

My section of ice detached from the chandelier. It probably made a horrible sound, but I heard nothing. Images came at me, loads of them: my mother pouring milk in expanding circles over a bowl of cereal, making sure every Cheerio got soaked; me laying on the carpet of my parent's home, reaching an arm underneath the sofa, trying to get a tennis ball that had somehow nestled itself beyond reach; me on stage with Justin at our first show at the Crocodile Café, thinking we'd finally made it and that the world would be nice to us.

Then I imagined how I looked from above, clinging to this mass of frozen water, fitted with axes, crampons, the harness, the rope. My mind even formulated some irony: the very objects I used to keep me attached and safe from harm now pulled me to my doom.

And like that, I tore free. Somehow, I still clutched both axes, hovering limp above the valley, spinning at the end of the rope. Below me, the falling ice gathered momentum as it flipped and spun down towards the bottom, crashing and breaking up.

It seemed like a long time hanging there before I felt myself being pulled up, a foot or so at a time, from above. Finally, I heard my name, though Justin had probably been yelling the entire time.

"Cory! Cory! You okay, man?" This was the first time I had ever heard him scared. His voice quaked almost as much as my body.

I clipped the axes to my waist belt and clenched the

rope in my hands, as if being cinched up the cliff would snap it when being ripped from the ice hadn't. I couldn't help it. I brought my legs up into my chest and surrounded the rope with my body like a fetus hunched around an umbilical cord.

~

Once Justin finished dragging me back up to the ledge, we climbed the most direct route up in a panic. The ascent felt absurdly slow, though I bet it was the fastest we'd ever climbed, despite the adrenaline shakes taking over my body and making us stop every five minutes. The muscles and tendons in my forearms and wrists felt like putty, and I could barely feel my hands from the shock of holding both axes so tight, but none of that prevented me from flying up the ice.

~

We sat on a boulder overlooking the valley with our legs draped over the side. The clouds had either dissolved or been scared away by the bright heat of the sun. The ice below spit and chattered every so often. Neither of us said anything. We just sat there, tired and empty. In some spots, Justin's face looked almost bruised. I'm sure mine appeared much worse.

"I can't believe we climbed this in May," I said, and swatted a green bottle fly from the crust of my mashed peanut butter and banana sandwich. I stuffed a moist bite into my mouth even though I wasn't hungry.

Justin took a few long gulps from his water bottle. "I

don't know man," he said. "This has got to be some sort of omen."

It sure seemed like one to me. "The last two years have been an omen," I said. "If not the last ten."

"What the fuck are you talking about?"

"I almost died there."

"Oh, come on." He threw an apple core over the ledge. "Of course that's how you'd take it. What you were doing was surviving."

It felt nothing like survival. I was done with driving our van around the country, waiting out hangovers in Wal-Mart parking lots, shifting debt back and forth between credit cards. Even our songs seemed the wrong kind of desperate. "This is how you're going to be?" I asked.

"As opposed to...?"

"You almost killed us."

"I almost killed us? You agreed to it. Don't forget that."

"It's not the same."

"Listen to yourself. You're like one of those anarchists who pays taxes."

"Just admit it. You fucked up."

"We're here, aren't we?"

"Barely. As always."

"What's that supposed to mean?"

He knew what it meant. I don't know why it was so difficult for me to just come out and say it when I'd already said it in so many other ways. But he refused to translate when I spoke in code. He treated anything less than straight confrontation as compliance—which, granted, it had always been.

The shakes galloped through my hands and chest. "It

means I'm done with the band," I said. "Everything."

He took a deep breath and wouldn't look at me for a second. "Bullshit."

"I mean it. I'm out. We played in Pratt, man. The Stoob Tavern. This shit's not going to get better."

"Just relax. You had a crazy experience. Give it a few days."

"A few days? I've given it years, and what's come of it? Nothing."

"That's a hell of a thing to say to the person who just saved your life."

"Saved it? This is exactly what I'm talking about. This is exactly why I can't do this anymore. I'm not the one who's nuts here. You drive this band into the ground and call it courage. I try to do the smart thing and it's painted as some sort of weakness."

He smiled and patted me on the back. Then he laughed aloud. "Finally! Nice work, Cory. I wondered when you were going to come out and say how you really felt. Ten point bonus. Advance to the next level."

"You see? There it is. So fucking condescending. Trying to cover up for the fact that you have no idea how to turn this thing around. You haven't a fucking clue. Do you."

He leaned back and let out a deep breath. "Here's the thing, Cory. You want me to say yes because you want this to work as much as I do, but you still—after thirteen years, for Chrissake—you still can't go there on your own. And what the hell are you going to do once we're done? Sell real estate? You're a guitar player, man. I'm a fucking singer, and for some reason you view any difficulties as disproving that fact. I'm trying to drive into that dense head of yours that we've played music for thirteen years, we are still playing music, and it's who we are. The only difference between us is that, unlike you, I'm okay riding out the low times."

"I'm done," I said.

"Take a breather," he said. "I'll see you at the bottom."

I watched him gather his gear and leave. I looked out over the side of the mountain and saw all the beauty, and I felt more tired than I'd ever been. I didn't care anymore what we did. I swallowed the rest of my crushed sandwich and washed down the peanut butter that had stuck to the top of my throat with a long drink of ice water.

~

When I caught up with Justin near the base of Mother of Pearl, the whole chandelier came down in front of us. Big pieces unhinged and toppled end-over-end, causing others to do the same. Then, with a blast, the rest of the ice plunged like someone had opened a trap door beneath it. The ground trembled. I don't know why, but we ran towards the ruin, even as sedan-sized chunks crashed down. Soon, everything lay jumbled at the bottom, and the waterfall pounded free onto thousands of tons of sweating ice.

Another jolt of adrenaline surged through me. I hunched over. My stomach felt terrible. I vomited the sandwich and the water, then bile until I was dry. I lay down on my back and breathed. "This is the omen."

Justin laughed. "You're fine. Stay here. I need to take some photos of what's left of this. Why the hell didn't I record it? "I closed my eyes.

~

The whole drive back to Seattle, Justin talked about our plans. He swore we could get some good press if we wrote an article about our climb up the falls and how close we'd come to dying. We could spin it into a resurrection story: nearly escaping death and rising like a phoenix. He said the pictures he'd captured of the aftermath and the one of me straddling the ice just before it fell were epic. Somewhere like *Spin* might publish it, maybe even *Outside*. And he knew someone who knew someone at *Rolling Stone*.

I didn't argue. My head ached, my hands and wrists throbbed, and my throat and stomach felt raw. It felt strange being back there in the van with him, riding shotgun, as usual, after all that had happened, after all I had said. Even with our equipment and belongings stuffed in the back, even though this had been my life for so long, it didn't feel like mine any longer. How many hours had I spent driving down the highway while Justin went on and on about every future possibility, no matter how minute? It didn't matter. I was a visitor.

"We'll start from scratch," he said. "Everything's changing anyway. I was watching this show the other day—did you know that even the polar ice caps are melting?"

I did.

Boy with the Unprotected Arm

Pencils behind ears, stats books in hand, the coaching staff crunched the numbers. Above, in the stands, parents crunched, too. In the announcer's booth, a couple of old, sturdy-jawed WASPs crunched live for the eyes and ears of the entire world. Everyone was hard at work, trying to find a way to prevent the boy with the unprotected arm from pitching the end of the final game of the Little League World Series.

From his spot on the bench, deep in the sunken dugout, Yaz—the boy with the unprotected arm—crunched the numbers as well, and he came to the same conclusion as everyone else. It was the bottom of the 14th inning, still a tie ballgame, and all the rest of the arms on the team—by league regulation—now stood under protection, sealed from the pitching mound, so as not to damage them prematurely. Their innings were spent. If any one of them hurled another pitch, the game would be forfeit.

He felt a pat on his back. It was Johnny, the catcher, whose face didn't hide his worry. Yaz looked past him down the bench and saw the rest of his teammates. None of them looked confident, either.

You see, dear reader, Yaz wasn't a pitcher. He wasn't much of a player, either. He was the head coach's son, used to non-competitive bench activities like chewing sunflower seeds, chatting nonsense to the opposing team's pitcher, and making up clever nicknames for everyone's mom.

Johnny got distracted and pointed at something, and Yaz saw, beyond the field, hovering over the center field wall, on the jumbo screen, something he'd never seen before—something he'd only ever imagined in his dreams. It stunned him. The thousands of LED lights were reproducing his own stumpy form. Those were his cheeks, shiny red and puffed squirrel-like with seeds. That was his rally cap turned inside out on top of his head.

It was then that Yaz became not just sure, but *sure* sure. He would pitch. Yaz was no dummy. Nor, dear reader, was he under the impression that his place on the team was anything other than pure nepotism, though he wouldn't have put it in those terms. Yaz didn't like the fact that he was only on the team because his dad was the coach, but he'd *come to terms with it*, as his therapist often said. Sure, at times, his comparative lack of skill filled his heart with a heavy blue sap. After all, his dad had played in the Major Leagues while the only trophies on the boy's shelf were for his work with the Young Thespians, which wasn't the same, at least not in his household.

And his parents named him after Red Sox great Carl Yastrzemski, for crying out loud. No pressure.

So sometimes, in the early morning and late at night, when his mind was soft and warm and without armor, the obvious questions searched Yaz: why did he have to be the proverbial apple that fell from the branches like a hanging curveball? Why did his Granny Smith have to smack so hard off his father's knobby wooden roots that it rolled all the way to a different orchard? Why couldn't he have been born more like his father?

It was frustrating to Yaz—at times, humiliating—but over the years, he'd survived and even flourished, because the tree his apple came to rest beneath fruited trickster charm by the bushelful. The boy with the unprotected arm was king of the dugout dirty joke, prince of the postgame card trick, master of the secret shaving cream puff on the lid of the oblivious power hitter's cap.

And his teammates loved him for it. In the dugout, he ruled.

But, dear reader, people with his skillset never got serious screen time on the ballpark Jumbotron during the Little League World Series. And for the last fifteen seconds—he'd been counting each tick—his mug had filled that jumbo screen like some titan of sport. His! It was a trip. He liked how he looked up there in the lights. It felt like something he could get used to. He almost forgot he had to pitch.

But then the screen blinked and began showing a player from the opposing team strutting out onto the field, a player whose apple had landed snugly within the mighty grove from which it fell. Hiro Yamamatsu III: grandson of Japan's all-time home run leader.

From the dugout, Yaz watched as the Minami Tigers' cleanup hitter prowled around inside the on-deck circle. The perfect miniature of his legendary patriarch took hungry swings with an orange-and-black Easton Power Brigade. He was hungry for fat pitches. Yaz's specialty.

"Don't look at him," interrupted Yaz's father. His muscular form blocked the screen from his son's view. "You've got this," he said. "Strike that kid out and send them all back to Japan."

Yaz nodded and tried to find some confidence in his father's encouragement, but there was precious little. He smelled the mint-flavored chewing tobacco on his father's breath and wished it didn't gross him out.

"Son," he continued, "you might not believe it, but I

know you've got it in there just waiting to emerge. Be a hero today."

A hero. Right. But he had no choice, so he squinted his eyes, pressed his protective cup tight, and stood up in the way he felt a champion would. For a moment, he willed a part of him to believe his father's words. Maybe this opportunity had arisen in order that he could finally show his stuff. Maybe he could be a hero. He doubted he could ever really sustain any level of success at baseball, but maybe he could get lucky. Maybe something magical would happen.

But the little confidence he'd mustered was short lived. As Yaz strutted out onto the field, chest artificially puffed, heart pounding, he crossed over the chalk lines and into the diamond, and the whole situation once again felt ridiculous. The Hollywood ending his father had just spewed, that he was going to triumph, that somehow, despite all his previous errors, all those seasons filled with snafus, his lifelong litany of hardball blunders, this moment would be different? Pure bull.

Yaz resumed walking to the mound. What sucked the most was that he realized how important this moment was to his father. Yaz doubted that his father would be able to laugh this failure off, as he had so many other of his son's attempts at sport because, for his father, arriving shortly was a moment more important than any other: the glory moment. Yaz was no dummy. He knew his father still harbored hope that he'd be a boy for whom those moments existed. He knew his father still hoped his son would be like him.

"Just feel it," he heard his father yell from the bench.

The smell of buttered popcorn blew in from the

stands. Yaz took a deep breath and climbed the mound. His fingers had become damp and sweaty and sticky on the inside of his glove. Feel it, his father had said. He'd been saying that to Yaz for what seemed like his entire life. Yaz blinked, shook his head, and took another deep breath. Feel what? Some sort of mystical strand of DNA hiding in his cells? Some lost key that could unlock the buff and quick and fast that had eluded him all this time?

Yaz felt the eyes of everyone in the stands watching his every move and wished he had pockets to stuff his hands into. He looked down at his cleats and pants and saw how dreadfully clean they were. He didn't belong here, and he never would. He knew that. He was not a pitcher—he was hardly even a player—and right then and there, the small, long-suffering part of his heart still holding out the hope that he might someday be like his father coughed once and croaked. He found the will to climb the small, dusty mound and stand up straight at the top. He kicked dust off the white rubber. He closed his eyes and thought, *Might as well get this over with.*

But when he opened his eyes and looked up, something had changed. The bright lights now seemed not overwhelming, but warm. The eyeballs on him didn't feel like threats; they seemed to beam goodness. And how had he missed the sheer pomp of it all, what with the signs and banners and cameras and, of course, the Jumbotron?

His ears popped and he heard voices hollering encouragement. It was just a handful, but they cheered for him. He'd never gotten the opportunity to perform for a crowd even a tenth this size with the Young Thespians, and yet, here he was. Maybe not on the stage he liked, but a stage, nonetheless. Maybe not under the circumstances he wanted, but still. This was a genuine moment.

He punched his glove with his fist, and a swell of applause burst from the crowd. He nodded again and received the same response. Then he thought to himself, *Why not?* and he lifted both his hands into the air, as if to say 'Behold! You have asked for the boy with the unprotected arm, and here he is! Enjoy!'

He began turning. He turned and turned, arms in the air, facing the crowd, all around, which—with his spinning—began to swell and then roar. The blink and shutter of thousands of cameras started to flicker with Morse code messages of love.

As he spun, he caught sight of his father by the dugout, waving his hands and yelling, "No! No!" He also glimpsed Hiro Yamamatsu III in the batter's box, shaking his head in disgust. They were disappointed. They were growing angry. But Yaz didn't care—not now. *Forget them*, he thought. *This is my moment. Not the next moment. They can have that one. And who cares if the entire world only treasures the next moment. This one—the moment before the moment—is all mine.* And Yaz kept spinning. After he stopped, he leapt from the mound and led the crowd in a round of The Wave. They loved it. They'd never seen anything like it.

Dear reader, the boy with the unprotected arm, Yaz, milked it. Because he was a smart boy, and he knew that, eventually, the umpire would come out and stop him, and he'd have to toe the rubber, wind up, thrust forward, and let that white globe spin end-over-end toward the plate, where he knew it would seek young Hiro Yamamatsu III's bat like a hot lover. Because in the end, pitches like his were meant for folks like the elder Hiro to crush; pitches like his were meant to be swatted deep into the upper deck by people like his own father; pitches like his were meant to help boys like Hiro Yamamatsu III triumph in their moments, those boys who had to miss all the fun dugout tricks due to all their pesky hitting and fielding responsibilities, those boys who could never understand the play of play ball, those serious boys who were still years from understanding what it's like to have no need for protection.

Last Night in Midlick

We get kicked out of the all-night bowling alley at three a.m. for trying to bowl with cabbages—a dare—so Caleb and I exit that dump for Midlick to break in and climb its water tower. We plan on throwing some balsa wood airplanes off the top—in junior high we came up with the idea—and paint a huge dick on the water bowl or whatever it's called. This will be a final installment of the epic shit we've been pulling all senior year.

The night is cool, and bugs *thip* against the windshield of Caleb's new white Chevy Silverado. My graduation cap and its asshat tassel sit in the backseat on top of my crumpled gown. We drive through the dark, headlights lighting the future or whatever. I check my phone and think about how fucking incredible it will be when word gets around that there's a dick over Midlick. We park down the hill from the tower. We walk through the long grasses already wet with dew. In our flashlight beams, crickets leap around, looking like little comets.

"I always thought of the water tower as an iron dildo," says Caleb.

"Pretty sure it's steel."

"And we've left the periodic table."

I hate it when Caleb gets clever. Sometimes I don't know what the fuck he's saying, and I think he enjoys that. We climb over the fence circling the tower, find the ladder at its base, and climb through the tart smell of corrugated steel and dry wind. When we reach the top, a few ducks scurry away, their webbed feet platting along the grated floor.

"What the fuck are ducks doing here?" I ask "Isn't this too high? I don't think of ducks as high fliers."

"Migration."

"Birds don't migrate in June."

"And some never migrate. They just come up here to get illicit."

I look down, and soon I'm trying not to. I can barely see the ground below, and something about that makes me hot and dizzy. "I'm kind of freaking out."

"Yeah man, it sucks about Meredith—"

"—it's not that." I broke up with my girlfriend Meredith last week. Hardest thing ever. I love her, but she's off to the East Coast for school in the fall, and I wanted to be the one to end it. She told me she hated me. Caleb thinks I'm stupid but won't say it. He and his Silverado don't get it. "I'm just caught between highs."

"You should get caught between thighs. Also, I have these," says Caleb, pulling a small Ziploc bag from the pocket of his jeans. "They'll bring down the paranoia."

We circle the tank and scatter the rest of the ducks, which make quiet honks and flap their wings before launching down into the dark. A breeze picks up, much colder than it had been on the ground. The wind sounds different up here, too—more busy, more free—like it's fucking gleeful to pass us by. Caleb sits down cross-legged and unzips the backpack.

"Just the Sour Diesel?" I ask.

"Yessir. Turn off your headlamp before liftoff."

I do, and the stars appear. "This Diesel tastes like Brussels sprouts. You'd think that with a cart they could get rid of it."

"It's not that bad."

"It's more that it doesn't have to be bad at all."

"Think of it this way," said Caleb. "From this day forward, should you ever taste Brussels sprouts, you will be reminded of when you graduated, got kicked out of a bowling alley, and climbed a water tower."

"Graduated?" I spit over the side of the guard rail. I noticed he didn't say anything about spray painting.

"I don't think it'll matter in the end. They let you walk with everyone. No one knows."

"Please. Everyone knows."

"Look, Brandon Townsend's ribs deserved cracking. He's such a pretentious asshole. He'll probably grow up to be president."

Sometimes Caleb reminds me of Brandon. I broke Brandon's ribs because he spoke his mind. Caleb probably thinks the same shit but keeps quiet. He's friendly to cover his cold heart. I don't really care. I've known this for years. Anyways, he'll be gone soon to college or university—I've never understood the difference.

I take a long pull on the pen. The tip lights up a bright, electric blue.

"See this darkness?" Caleb asks. "We're going to fill it with light."

He reaches back into the backpack. Like I was saying, we hatched this plan to throw planes off the water tower in junior high. No bullshit symbolism, just the fulfillment of an old promise. In the lamplight, we slide balsawood parts from the plastic sleeve and thread the wings through the body.

"Where are the LEDs?" he asks.

I hand him two buttons, take my own, and press them onto either side of the cockpit for balance. We turn off our lamps and face the horizon. Miles to the east, the city glows.

"This may be as high as we'll ever get," I say, but he doesn't respond.

In silence, at the same time, we throw. The planes circle, dive, and stall, wind pushing them sideways, LED lights leaving trails of red. I lose track of Caleb's plane. Mine goes down in the tall grasses below, and you can just see its lights blinking like little alarm clocks.

We're quiet. I have the spray paint, but a part of me knows Caleb won't want to go ahead with it. He would have done it a few months ago, but he's changed. 'Too much heat,' he'll say. He doesn't realize how cold it can get, and how heat can warm a person. I grab the spray paint and shake the bottle, so it rattles. Caleb pretends not to hear. He already thinks that just by being here, he's doing me a favor. Like the school allowing me to wear the graduation gown to save face. I take it.

I Never Heard Your Voice

A clothes dryer needs zippers and coins to find its voice. Spinning, the metal lives, crackling and spitting like drops of water into a frying pan. I imagine opening the door to fledgling songbirds flying out, chirping like metal-struck coins to each other from the backs of their tiny throats. My own young songbirds have already bedded down, little balls with beaks pulled back beneath their wings. They slide through the dreams of the living. What I hope of dreams is to lead my hands through warm clothes toward what I seek, which isn't loud money or silver teeth but the quiet feathers of the one who passed. The sound lives in my mind, grows feathers, flies through my teeth every time I praise my children, every time I tell them their father loves them, every time they try to fly before they're ready, like the one I'll never meet.

Good Morning, Sweetheart

"We just assumed," Craig says.

His infant daughter slept so much, as all do, and when awake, appeared as though she could see.

We both look down at the bundle of pink still curled in her car seat resting in the chair adjacent to our table. Waiters bustle through the patio with stacked plates while dozens of conversations swell and taper around us.

"She made eye contact?" I ask.

"Sure," he says. "We'd talk to her, and she'd look straight at us. The dog would bark, and she'd turn."

"But it wasn't—"

"No. That was just her hearing us."

I sip my soda and watch him watch her. "Just take Craig out to lunch and give him a little encouragement," my wife Emma had said. "Let him know he's going to be a great father." And she reminded me that he'd wanted to be one for so long—that they'd tried for so long. She said that now he blames himself for her eyes.

"I feel terrible not knowing sooner," says Craig.

"How could you have?"

"I know, I know. But we should have done the modern thing. It was there in my mind. I thought about it. But Molly and I had these ideas." He leans back and scrapes his fingernails through his hair. "We wanted it to be natural. You know? Just us and her."

"Sure. Of course," I say. I get it. I'm a doctor and am used to all of it—the machines, the graphs, the blips, all the uniforms rushing in and rushing out, all the dull metallic instruments peeled from airtight wrappers.

He leans back in. "Could they really have caught it? You know, if we'd done the modern thing?"

"Probably not," I say, meaning not right away. They most likely would have in follow-ups, perhaps early on. But why tell him? At his daughter's age, in the few early months we're talking about, knowing wouldn't have made much of a difference, especially in an attentive family like his own. And anyways, my wife Emma is right: what he really wants are more avenues through which he can feel the blame. I've seen this before in the parents of my patients, and I can't find any fault in it. When something goes wrong with a child that young—your child—you want to take that hurt away and make it your own.

Lunch arrives. We pick at our sandwiches. His daughter stirs in the car seat when a group at the table across from us erupts in laughter. He leans over, whispers something to her, and she calms down. When he looks back up, I see pain in his forehead, in the corners of his mouth, in his eyes.

"Craig," I say. "You did just fine. And you couldn't have done anything different, even if you had known."

"We just weren't looking for it."

"Of course not. "Why would you?"

He takes a sip of water and clears his throat. "We found out last Saturday. We were out with her stroller in the sun, and she didn't squint." He picks up his sandwich and puts it right back down. "But this is what gets me," he says, looking at his daughter again. "Even before then, we talked about it. Molly wondered. She had that intuition. But we didn't do anything. I told her she was being dramatic. I know. It's terrible. We were both so tired."

"I might have said the same thing. And anyways, sleep

deprivation makes you crazy."

"But do you know why I told Molly that she was being dramatic? Do you know how I convinced her everything was okay?" He handles his sandwich and stuffs a stray piece of lettuce back underneath the bread. Again, he looks at his daughter. "She smiled."

"You mean–"

"Yeah. She smiled at us. We'd say, "Good morning, sweetheart," and she'd smile back at us and laugh. I told Molly there was no way she would do that if...you know. No way."

"Of course."

"But then, when we finally went to the doctor, do you know what he said?"

I shake my head.

"No offense, but the prick said it was a survival response. Nothing more. He said even blind children smile so that their parents will grow attached to them. Survival. That's it." With his fork, Craig spears a cut of melon in the small fruit bowl next to his plate.

I don't know what to say. I suspect the doctor was only trying to do then precisely what I'm trying to do now. Craig just can't see it.

He leaves his fork in the melon and looks at his daughter. He reaches over to touch her feet, but she wriggles and stretches out, one arm above her head, fist clenched, and grunts. "I can't believe he said that," says Craig. "A survival response. Like there's no us and her. Like there's nothing between us."

I am about to explain to him what the doctor probably meant when his daughter smacks her lips and begins blinking her eyes. I watch Craig's face soften and his shoulders relax. He looked so burdened a moment ago.

"Good morning, sweetheart," he says.

She opens her gummy mouth wide and smiles, then reaches out her arms, grasping for more assurance of what she will never see.

He picks her up and holds her with his left arm, tight against his shoulder, and closes his eyes.

The Meme

On the night of September 5th, 2020, at the height of the pandemic, I received an email from my pastor, Richard Schuman, containing a humiliating, ableist meme of me that would ruin both our lives. The meme portrayed me speaking at our church's monthly lecture series on the world Jesus lived in. The picture was a jpeg of me, Francis Barrett, mid-sentence, Adam's apple like a baby's fist, jawbone sharp and unevenly set, head tilted slightly to the left, mouth partially open, teeth vaguely yellow, thin hair previewing my impending baldness. My navy-blue blazer hid the lower third of a red tie with a knot in need of straightening. Overall, to be blunt, I looked like I was having a spasm. I have a speech impediment that forces me to read my lectures line-by-line, straight from the page, rather than to simply work with notes or an outline. Written across the top of the meme was a series of incoherent words meant to emulate someone like me—'fuh fuh duh duh doy doy'—you know, that awful kind of thing. The jpeg was embedded in the email, and above were three crying-with-laughter emojis.

There, in my third floor, one-bedroom apartment in the University District of Seattle, wearing flannel pajamas and sitting back against the headboard, phone in palm, I nearly spilled my evening bourbon on my lap. I rushed to my desk across the room, flipped open the laptop, and saw the meme in larger size. Was this how Richard saw me?

No. I couldn't believe it. I immediately made excuses for him. He was younger than me, and I knew younger millennials could be irreverent sometimes. Most importantly, he was a pastor, a man of character, so he couldn't really mean anything by it. How could he? Along with my speech impediment, I struggle with a serious mood disorder, most often residing in the category of depression, and Richard knew that. Two weeks before he sent me the meme, I'd shared my struggles with him—struggles which had worsened over the pandemic—and asked him to remember me in his prayers. He agreed and even went so far as to ask me if he could share what I was going through with his wife, so that she could pray, as well. So this incongruence of the meme—that he, of all people, would knowingly hurt someone when they were down—didn't make sense.

I made more excuses. I figured he'd probably been tipsy; sometimes he'd send these late-night, passionate emails to the ministry team out of nowhere, making points that didn't need to be made. You could hear the slurring through the typed words. I suspected that most of us—like me—were drinking through the pandemic in an attempt to keep sane. He deserved some grace.

I reminded myself that I was sensitive to a fault. I'd always been that way. Things didn't brush off me like they did for others. It was my problem that I was offended. A part of me even felt, well, flattered that he was even thinking of me at all. I thought that maybe this is just how he treats his friends. Now I might fit that definition.

Is it strange to say I felt closer to him? I've learned that cruelty is a form of intimacy, forced on people whether they like it or not, and in my loneliness, I don't know that I minded it as much as you might think. I should have minded it on principle, but I wasn't at a place to hold my principles higher than my need for community.

Truthfully, I'd been bullied before, many times, so I had a high tolerance for it, even though it had been years.

I replied with one crying-with-laughter emoji and "Hah! Thanks for that." Then I slugged down the bourbon and poured myself another glass.

~

Richard continued to send me the memes monthly, a day or two after my lectures. In my weekly meetings with my therapist, Dani, a non-binary fifty-something, Richard kept coming up in conversation without me even realizing it. The more I talked with them about the situation, the more I realized how confused and upset I was. One day, we met at their office downtown, both of us in masks, sun streaming through the windows and warming my back. I sat on the couch while they sat in a wicker chair with a lime green cushion, wearing their usual: Birkenstocks, tight black jeans, and a colorful blouse, their auburn hair in a pixie cut. They asked me what I thought might happen if I talked to Richard about the memes.

"I don't know. I-I've never seen him confronted by anyone before, or ever mention it happening. I guess he sometimes talks about mistakes he's made in the past, s-s-s-so I know it has happened." I felt guilty talking poorly about Richard behind his back.

"Do you think it would be a good idea?" They set their laptop down on the coffee table and slid their legs beneath them on the chair. This was a sign they were ready to move from discussing my symptoms, which needed to be tracked, to the part of our sessions where we explored what was on my heart.

"Maybe. Y-Yeah. Probably."

"Then what's stopping you? I mean that as a question, not a challenge. What is it, precisely, that is keeping you, and has kept you, from letting him know how it makes you feel?"

"I don't know. I j-j-just feel like, if I understood why he is doing it, it would be okay."

"Do you think this should be okay?"

"I know it's not. But I don't know—" I said, trailing off. What if Richard took it the wrong way? "I can't burn this bridge. I f-f-feel like the church is all I've got."

They blinked a few times and squinted. I knew they wanted to say that it wasn't worth it—that I should get out, that this was fucked up—but they wanted me to come to that on my own. They knew I deferred to other people's opinions way too much, which is one of the reasons I had gotten into this situation in the first place.

This sense of belonging was important because, as the pandemic dragged on, admissions plummeted at the progressive seminary where I taught church history, and it had recently closed its doors. I didn't want to try and find another seminary job in a different city because the pandemic made building new, in-person relationships nearly impossible. As I mentioned, I had a strong community at Richard's church which—importantly—had a large young adult ministry. For people like me, young adult ministries were the best place to find a spouse. I hadn't given up looking to marry a woman who shared my faith. I was 38, older than most of the attendees, but they didn't hold it against me. On top of that, I was already profoundly depressed. It was difficult enough for me to leave the house, much less change my life, so I applied for local jobs. The week before, I'd accepted one at the tech company *Coaster* as a copyeditor which, though boring and mostly remote, paid as well as the seminary.

Dani nodded. "It makes sense that you don't want to burn bridges. But I have a challenge for you. I want you to try to access the pain that you feel more deeply. I know that you pray. Perhaps as a start, you pray that you can feel it, then wait and be mindful. Let's try for a few minutes. Do you want any ice?" If I was very anxious, sometimes Dani would go to the office kitchen and get me two ice cubes to squeeze in my hands over a trash bin; extremes in temperature were a good way to reset one's mind.

"I think I'm okay w-w-without it." I bowed my head, closed my eyes, and tried to pay attention to my body. My pulse had quickened, as had my breath. I tried to feel the fears, like they said, but it was confusing and unsettling. I was like a dolphin chasing a school of fish in a nature documentary I'd seen. The moment I approached, they'd all scatter. After a few minutes, I opened my eyes. "It's hard."

"You don't need to figure this all out today," they said. "Spend some time doing it at home. But Francis, I want to throw this out there: maybe Richard needs to hear this. I would call what he's doing bullying, even abuse. You say he's otherwise a nice guy. Maybe this will be a gift to him. All of us have our blind spots. Maybe he'll change, and the same thing won't happen to someone else."

Dani thought I was being bullied, an idea I rejected at once. Abuse? I'd put up with bullies all throughout school, but they were most, if not all, malicious—none of them were nice, like Richard. I wondered if I'd given him enough credit in my sessions with Dani, if I'd portrayed an accurate picture, if I'd intentionally misled them, accidentally making this bigger than it really was through my insecurity. I wondered if my need for compassion from them was misshaping the truth.

But the question remained: Why was he doing this, and why to me? I concluded that I had to know, regardless of whether the behavior stopped or not.

~

I met Richard at a coffee shop just past the north end of Seattle—one that was black-owned, one the church had given money to help start. Richard's church had some of the trappings of a megachurch—like a rock band instead of a choir, movie theater seating instead of pews, and a younger crowd—but it also had an intellectual bent. There in line, Richard wore tan Carhart pants, a gray North Face t-shirt with a silhouette of a mountain, and a retro Mariners cap. He would fit in anywhere in the Pacific Northwest as a basic, normal, middle-to-upper-middle-class white person, just like almost everyone else in the church—including me—only slightly more rugged. And gentle at the same time. It's tough for me to describe him. There are some people you can see and understand quickly and others who are elusive. But he looked you in the eyes when he talked, and when you talked, he squinted a bit, as if he were really listening hard to what you were saying. There are very few people who make me feel as if they really want to know me rather than just acting polite.

He greeted the manager—a rail-thin twenty-something with a faux hawk—and she came around from behind the counter and gave him a big hug.

"Free coffee for this guy," she said.

"Give it to the person behind me," he said, meaning me.

We sat down near the window, and he asked how my preparations for my next lecture were going. He told me about one of his son's select soccer experiences—how intense it was, how youth soccer was becoming less of a sport and more of a lifestyle. He took a sip of his coffee and smiled at me. "So, to what do I owe this pleasure?"

"I have something I want to d-d-discuss with you." I'd rehearsed this conversation in my head countless times, feeling each one. I was no longer prescribed benzodiazepines for sleep due to my passive suicidality, so I had been awake all night, trying to distract myself with television, books, internet games and videos—you name it. I was exhausted.

"Sure thing. Is this ministry related?"

"Well, it's more p-personal."

"Good. Good. I get so tired of talking church business all the time. I feel like I never get the chance to really know the people who attend and serve as volunteers."

I took a small sip of coffee. I felt lightheaded. "It's about the m-m-memes you send me after my lectures."

He grinned and leaned back in his chair, resting his hands on his lap. "Hah! You like those?"

"Well, that's the thing. It's not that I don't think they're funny in their own way. I just don't understand why you do them. Sometimes I think, w-w-well, that I'm kind of a joke to you."

He looked shocked. "No, no, no! Not at all. I have a deep respect for you. You know the Bible better than I do, for crying out loud. No, I just think you have one of those faces."

"What do you mean?"

"Like, you have these, I don't know, expressions. You have such an expressive face. I was telling my wife that you could be a character actor. Like someone on Saturday Night Live. Like a Steve Buscemi. It's fantastic."

"But the c-c-caption, with me, you know..."

"Oh, that's all part of what I'm saying. It's just a joke. I thought you'd get a kick out of it. You've never seemed like a guy who took himself too seriously. I do these memes for a handful of folks who aren't all uptight like a lot of the people at church."

"It's just that, well, it makes me feel uncomfortable. I'm not s-s-saying you're a bad person..."

He waited for me.

"Well, it's like this. I've worked in churches before. Most p-p-people don't take this kind of joke very well. And if the elders and staff at the church were to see these, knowing what I've been going through, well, they would think it was inappropriate."

He blinked. "Is that a threat?"

"N-n-no, not at all. I'd never do that. But it's just, if you are doing this to people, and it gets out, you'd be in big trouble. Like s-s-say someone gets mad at you and posts it on Facebook and tags you and the church...you could lose your job."

He stared at me, squinting, scanning my face. "Okay, okay. I'll stop. I can respect that. You're probably right." He leaned back and stretched, but the move looked, in hindsight, contrived. "Thanks for the insight. I consider you a friend, and you've done what friends do: offer wise counsel."

"Thank you." I felt relieved, to say the least. I almost felt like crying. I wanted to hug him, to apologize for even bringing it up.

He checked his phone. "Hey, someone needs me. I have to go, but thanks for this."

We both left, him to his Subaru Outback, me to my Toyota Corolla. At home, I felt good about it, so much so that I emailed Dani, and they emailed me right back with "Wonderful! This is a big step. I'm so glad you're being more assertive. Let's talk more about it in our next session." I went on a walk that night, singing worshipful songs under my breath and praising God. Richard had called me a friend, and I'd helped him avoid a potential pitfall. The opposite of what I'd feared happened. We'd become closer.

~

A week later, I received an email from Richard's secretary telling me that the ministry meeting about the lecture series had been canceled. A few days after that, she sent an email out to the ministry saying that the elders of the church had decided to go a different direction with the event; they were now going to hold monthly prayer and healing services instead. It said that the needs of the community had changed. I was disappointed and immediately feared it was because of our conversation.

After his sermon the next Sunday, I approached him as he was gathering his notes from the lectern.

He looked up and smiled. He wore black Converse All Stars, tight blue jeans, and a royal blue t-shirt with a thick, lime-green band—the t-shirt a nod to the fact that the Seahawks had an afternoon game in a few hours. "Francis. Franky. Frank-man. So good to see you. Hey, I'm sorry the elders changed the event. There are a lot of people still hurting in the aftermath of the pandemic whose pain isn't being addressed, and we feel called to fill that need. You understand. You've been through a lot yourself."

"Yes. I j-j-just wanted to thank you for the opportunity over the last few years. It's really m-m-meant a lot to me."

"It's meant a lot to me, too. Hey, I have to get to a meeting. Let's catch up sometime soon, okay?"

"Sounds good."

Is there a better feeling than that first sense of peace when a conflict is resolved? Is there a better feeling than that cool relief, besides love? I stuck around at the potluck after church and stayed to the very end; I even helped clean up. Richard had acted normally, perhaps with more warmth than usual, and had asked me to catch up, so it truly wasn't about me. He'd said that in a sermon before, that humans have the tendency to make everything about them when, in reality, it rarely is. He said we must keep our focus on Christ—it's Him who lives through us; if we follow ourselves, it will only lead us to pain.

But a week later, at ten on a Tuesday, I received a phone call from the associate pastor in charge of the young adult ministry—a tall guy with slicked back hair and an undercut who wore tight, highwater jeans and flannel shirts opened two buttons down, showing his collar bone. I could hear voices in the background of the phone; he was probably just out of a church meeting. He told me that it was time to move on from the young adult group at church. He told me I was the oldest person there—now

39—and they'd decided in the session meeting to make a hard age limit of 35. They didn't want to make the younger women uncomfortable. No one had mentioned my name, specifically, but there was a general sense among them that there needed to be some adjustments.

"I know you understand," he said. "You're a critical part of this church, and we want you involved. Maybe spend some time just being a pew sitter for a little while, pray for a new vision on where to go next in your volunteer ministry."

I hung up the phone and felt not disappointed, but confused, embarrassed, and ashamed. Was this because of me? Of what I had said? My therapy appointment with Dani was at noon, so I drove to their office and told them right away.

They paused for a moment, considering what I'd said. It was windy outside, and rain dripped down the windows.

"Do I need to be worried?" I asked.

"How involved are you there now?"

"Well, I'm not, really. I only g-g-go to services on Sunday."

They paused again and looked up, mouth pursed, as if they were thinking whether they should say anything and how they should say it. Finally, they said, "I don't know. I don't really know church culture that well, so you probably have a better gauge on this than I do. But I think you need to be prepared for the possibility that you're being pushed out. I'm sorry, Francis."

This stunned me. I was unable to speak for a few minutes. Dani handed me the tissue box and waited. I often depended upon Dani for clarity in situations I didn't understand. As a rule, I doubted myself and my ability to perceive a situation honestly. Part of this is my mood disorder. There's always this doubt in my mind: am I seeing this scenario for what it is, or is it distorted by my depression?

In the end, it didn't matter. I still attended on Sundays, but I couldn't help catastrophizing. Were there women there at that moment who I'd creeped out? Did Richard now hate me? Was I considered a wolf among the sheep? The building paranoia was too much, so a few weeks later, I left the church. No one followed up to see why I'd left or how I was doing. Silence.

After work, every night, for the better part of a year, I festered over it. Now that I wasn't in any sort of leadership position that demanded I stay sober, I drank with authority. I grew heavier, less attractive than I already was, and gave up on finding someone. I stopped reading the Bible and praying, angry with God that this was happening. I stopped going to therapy with Dani, despite her urging against my decision to quit. I blamed them for suggesting that I have that conversation with Richard. I decided, in response to all of this, that my only option was to meet every need for pleasure that my paycheck would allow. Once it was done, if my body didn't give out, I would crush all my pills, swallow them, and bid farewell.

But I didn't only wither. I grew angry at Richard with a dark energy. I wanted to send the photos to the elders at the church to get back at him. A human being must decide, over and over in their life, whether to seek justice or to protect others from what they've done. I could be like Jesus—like Richard so often urged us to—but which Jesus? The one giving mercy so gently that it might spark change? Or a severe mercy, hard as flint but able to spark that same change just as effectively? And what would each decision do to me?

The arguments didn't matter, in the end. One night, I was angry and depressed, and I drank myself into a fury. I know now why my temptation to drink is so strong: I feel powerless so often that being drunk is the only state in which I have enough of an ego to feel like my heart is worth defending. Sometimes there's a cost, though, and there was that night. I wrote a letter explaining my mental illness, my speech impediment, my involvement in the church, what Richard had done, and then my being pushed out. I pasted it into an email and attached every meme Richard ever made of me, as well as screenshots of the emails to prove I hadn't made them myself. I titled the email "Beloved Local Pastor Bullies Suicidal Volunteer Throughout the Pandemic" and sent it to *The Stranger* and *The Seattle Times*—I don't actually remember that part, but when I woke up around noon the next day, I had replies from both newspapers saying they were going to do some research and try to find others to interview; if it all checked out, they would run the story as soon as possible. I tried to convince them otherwise, but it was too late. They shared the articles, and the rest of the nation soon picked up the story, as well. It was only by seeing those pictures on the screen beneath the header of the *New York Times* that I realized how incredibly cruel Richard was for sending those pictures of me.

As the attention grew more intense, I also realized how foolish it was for me to make it public in the way I had. Somehow people got my phone number and email address, and I received dozens of messages—some of them requests to speak or appear or be interviewed, others of them making fun of me. I drank and drank and avoided the computer and my phone, but I never could keep away for long. It felt, at times, like I was reading my own obituary over and over. To some, I was a hero; to others, I was a joke. I didn't know who I was anymore, either. In the eyes of the world, I realized, I'd now been defined by the very photos that I hated the most. I could have erased them, but in revenge, I'd done the opposite. Only too late, I realized that what I wished didn't exist would never go away. I'd be defined not just as a victim, but as someone sad, inept, unable to defend himself. Weak. I'd let it go on for too long.

Two weeks after it came out, I made my way to a bridge and stood looking over the side. Soon cars had stopped, and I was being pulled back from the guard rail. Then the police arrived. A few hours later, I found myself in the inpatient hospital ward. I was there two months and was nurtured by the staff and counselors, as well as others like me. Once I had improved enough and was able to get some distance from the entire situation, I realized that I needed to change my own life and not depend on people like Richard to do it for me. I stopped drinking for good. I moved from my apartment near the north end of the city into the quiet, middle-class suburbs to the south. I grew a beard and always wore a hat. I closed all my email accounts, changed my phone number, changed my name, and got a job doing paperwork for a shipping company outside the city. I bought a software program that would allow me to block any website that might say something about me or was connected in any way to my previous life. I read news only from Europe where my story had less traction and avoided those from the States.

Instead of trying to find another church, I attended a mindfulness gathering every week. I would go on long retreats where, in the silence, I could feel the emotions inside of me slowly, slowly, begin to dissipate. I attended three group therapy meetings every week and volunteered often at the homeless shelter downtown. I soon felt part of a community of people who were like me. While volunteering, I met LeeAnne, a transplant from the south who reminded me of Dani in her warmth. I felt I could trust her enough to tell her what had happened, and she accepted me completely. She'd been bullied as a teenager, so she understood what it was like. We grew close but decided never to become romantic with each other. I'd given up on those sorts of relationships, and we weren't attracted to each other in that way, which was its own gift. She's still my closest friend.

One night, a few years later, while we were watching *PBS Newshour* in her apartment on a Friday night, I decided I was ready.

"Are you sure?" LeeAnne said. She swept her hair from her shoulder and leaned forward on her La-Z-Boy.

I closed my eyes and took a deep breath. "It's time."

"I believe in you."

She handed me her laptop. I sat down, took another deep breath, and tried to find Richard. I had to sift through a lot of articles, and as I saw the memes and read my name over and over again, I could feel that old discomfort, confusion, and pain in my chest. LeeAnne could tell I was distressed and came over and sat next to me. It seemed that Richard had never given an interview— never publicly apologized. There was only the statement of the church which has since changed its name and location, just like I did. I found his wife on Facebook, though. Her account was private, but I could still see the profile pic which was her with another man who was much taller than Richard, but dressed like him. He looked, well, dorky and trustworthy. Whether that was true, I could no longer tell. I have trouble trusting men.

After some more digging, I found him on X, of all places. His profile photo was a meme of a donkey and elephant fighting, and his posts were mean-spirited, belligerent, and sometimes attacked the church in all its forms. He had a large following, which wasn't surprising, given his gift for language and people. But that cruel part of him that sent me those memes was still there. I scrolled through his posts and read parts to LeeAnne.

"Should I message him?" I asked.

She put her hand on my shoulder. "Honey, you have to. For you."

I quickly made an account so that I could reply. I typed:

> Dear Richard,
> This is Francis. I want you to know that I forgive you for what you did, and I hope you will forgive me for my part in it. I would like to talk to you, whether in person or over the phone. I know I have a lot to say, and I'm guessing you might, too.
> Best wishes.

I left my phone number. I watched the message for a little while and was notified that he had seen it. I waited for nearly an hour for a reply, but received nothing. I checked it incessantly over the next few days with no luck. When I logged on about a week later, I discovered I had been blocked. A few days later, though, I got a phone call from a 616-area code—western Michigan—and, though I figured it was a spam call, I knew from his account that he lived in Grand Rapids, so I took the call.

"Is this Francis?"

I recognized him immediately, but his voice glistened, as if drunk. "Yes. Is th-th-this Richard?"

"Still got that pathetic stutter, I see. You know, most people can get over that. You probably keep it so you can get people's pity."

"I, I, I d-d-don't know what you're talking—"

"Whatever. It doesn't matter. I don't really want to talk to you. I just want you to know that you ruined my life. You and your sensitive, precious little heart. You ruined my marriage, my career, my family. Everything. I want you to live with that. I want that to seep into your bones and haunt you forever."

He hung up before I could reply.

I remember a story he told one Sunday morning from the pulpit. He talked of a friend he once knew who was a devoted Christian in college, one who took up partying hard in his fraternity. Soon after, the friend couldn't stand to go to the church anymore because he felt so guilty. Eventually this friend hated the church for judging him, and began to hate God for the same reason, when all the while what he truly hated was himself. He committed suicide, Richard said, because he believed in God but didn't believe in himself enough to follow him. Too simple of an answer, I realize now.

I don't know whether I will ever hear from him again.

I have no plans to search for him, at least not now, but I'm not so foolish as to think I never will. Sometimes I imagine him calling me and making plans to go to the coffee shop to tell the truth to each other. I imagine what it would be like if he started another church, knowing what he knows now—a church led by someone who understands what it means to be cruel and what can happen when we use our power to take liberties, to bully. I imagine us sitting next to each other in front of a congregation and telling our painful stories. I imagine redemption. I still have hope, which is part of how I got into this situation in the first place. I hoped I was wrong about Richard, hoped to the point of delusion, hoped to the point of betraying myself.

For the most part, I've moved on. Occasionally I see the memes, and they don't affect me the way they used to. But the truth is, I've had times of peace, but I've never felt free. I don't even know what that would feel like anymore.

I believe our dark, painful, unredeemed stories have their own desire apart from our will. They become weary of being tragic. I believe they want to arc toward the light and resolve into it. That's why the dark stories replay over and over. Those memories want us to help them reach the light and then become it. It's the reason we need photographs and friends: to bring forth the good memories—they've left us, already having found their homes, but the dark ones remain, unsettled, restless. They arise as pain, again and again, in our bodies and in our minds. They want to be free. Only then can they free us.

Acknowledgments

I'd like to express my heartfelt thanks to Robert P. Kaye, Jodi Paloni, and Mary Stein for their insight into these stories over the years, as well as to Erik Evenson, Len Kuntz, Christine Texeira, Ruth Schemmel, and Grant Ivison-Lane for their notes and encouragement along the way. I'm grateful to editors Josh Dale, Chanel Martins, and the whole Thirty West masthead for their tireless work and belief in my stories. I'm also grateful to Lori Hettler for her expertise in publicizing this book. I'm indebted to my teachers and workshop leaders David Jauss, Nance Van Winckel, Abby Frucht, Clint McCown, Trinie Dalton, Jess Row, Michael Byers, and Anthony Doerr. Thanks to Miles Wray at *Spartan*, one of the best editors out there, as well as M. Wong and C.K., who have had a profound influence on my thinking and life. To my parents, who have supported me and encouraged my love of literature since childhood, I'm beyond grateful. Finally, to Jess, Naomi, & Gus—your love & presence sustain me.

Grateful acknowledgment is also made to the following magazines, in which earlier versions of these stories first appeared:

Shenandoah: "Below the Falls"

Maudlin House: "Breakup Sketch

Virginia Quarterly Review: "Tonight We Are Kings"

Doctor T.J. Eckleburg Review: "Small Fiery Blooms"

The Adroit Journal: "First Rain"

Green Mountains Review: "The Island"

The Journal of Compressed Creative Arts: "Lap Lane"

Redivider: "Fit to Scale"

Post Road Magazine: "Libidonomics"

[PANK]: "What Happens"

JMWW: "Togetherness"

X-R-A-Y: "Glass"

Fiddleblack: "The Keeper of Strays"

Cease, Cows: "Tusks"

Five South: "The Failure"

Folio: "American Ice"

Stymie Magazine: "Boy with the Unprotected Arm"

Flash Frog: "Last Night in Midlick"

Tin House's Open Bar: "Good Morning, Sweetheart"

About the Author

Ross McMeekin is the author of a noir, *The Hummingbirds* (Skyhorse Publishing, 2018.) His short fiction has appeared in literary journals and magazines such as *Virginia Quarterly Review*, *Shenandoah*, *Redivider*, and *X-R-A-Y*. He has won fellowships from Hugo House and Jack Straw Cultural Center in Seattle. For the last ten years, he has served as editor of the literary journal, *Spartan*.

About the Publisher

Follow us on:

Scan the QR code to visit www.thirtywestph.com

Printed in the USA
CPSIA information can be obtained
at www.ICGtesting.com
LVHW090321220424
778050LV00006BA/424

9 798989 542215